Contents

PN
STORY WORLD

THE KAASHI

AN IMMORTAL LAND IN THE UNIVERSE

VOLUME 1: SCOUT

NARISHAN

Preface

My recent trip to the ancient city of Kaashi sparked something profound within me. It was there, amidst its timeless echoes, that the idea for this novel truly took root. I felt a strong pull to bring the incredible, supernatural side of Indian mythology back to life, and to introduce a new hero with extraordinary powers to our world. This book is my way of sharing that vision with you. My pen name is Narishan.

As I wrote, I was constantly astonished by the sheer greatness of Indian mythology and its countless stories. Even as someone who has loved mythology since childhood, my research for this novel opened my eyes to so much I never knew. Learning about the characters and the rich history of India helped me understand the unique beauty of Its cultural heritage in a whole new way. This journey of discovery, filled with unexpected insights, became as much a part of the book as the story itself.

This is a suspenseful mythological fiction, and I want you to be ready for a world full of surprises. Not just for you, the reader, but for the characters themselves. As you turn these pages, prepare to travel alongside them and discover the true essence of this story. My hope is that you approach this new fictional world, built around Kaashi and the greatness of Lord Shiva, with an open mind. Let go of any ideas you might have about mythology, and allow yourself to be fully immersed in this fresh experience.

This story began with a simple idea: a person completely unaware of Kaashi's existence, whose destiny has other plans, leading them on a quest to find their way there and uncover its secrets. With this novel, I wanted to share the knowledge and ideas I gained during this writing journey with you, almost like a friendly conversation.

Finally, I want to express my deepest gratitude to those who made this book possible. To my parents, for believing in me, supporting my passion, and letting me follow my dreams. To my little sister, for her unwavering help and for standing by me through everything. To my friends, for their constant support and for offering the criticism that helped shape my ideas and stories. A special thank you to B. Raghavendra Kumar and Vangara Aditya, who were with me from the very beginning, helping to shape this story, conduct essential research into Indian mythology, and develop the characters and plot twists. Despite their own busy lives, they dedicated their time to this project and been strong pillars in bringing this story to you. And to Satya Gopal and B.Sathvik, for their invaluable help with editing and critical suggestions that truly enhanced the final feel of the story. Finally to the team of Notion Press who helped me in bringing this story from the paper on my desk to the book in your hands.

I hope you enjoy reading this novel as much as I enjoyed creating it.

Embark on a Whimsical Jungle Adventure with Momo, the Monkey!

Chapter 1

The Kalabhairava

Varanasi Railway Station, 1998

Platform No. 2.

I sat alone under the cool, pleasant sky. My fingers numb with the weight of my thoughts, clamping tight around the edge of my ticket.

The railway station is quite chaotic with all kinds of people and the screeching of arriving trains, the rhythmic call of chai wallahs ("Chai! Chai!"), the stale metal tang mingling with the sweet, heavy scent of cheap incense seemed to recede and soften at the edges.

The world around me dissolved into indistinct shapes, irrelevant and distant, as my mind drifted through a tangled maze of memories and unanswered questions.

"You looked dazed and puzzled. Sharing worries can calm your mind." an old man who just came and sat beside me said in English. His voice was so calm yet piercing, talking to me as if he had known me for a long time.

"What happened, young man? What's bothering you so much? People usually visit this place either to give their loved ones a final send off or visit the god here… you look like you come here for neither of them."

I didn't look up immediately. My eyes were still fixed on the ticket in my hand, my thoughts still adrift. After a pause, I replied, "You're right. I do not belong to this country, but I am native to this land and here is my origin. I don't know who I am… but many in this country seem to know what I am."

My voice trailed off into the silence. Then something shifted inside me a sudden jolt, as if I had been woken from a dream. I turned to the old man, my eyes searching for him, and I asked softly, "May I know who you are to ask these questions?"

He didn't answer right away. Instead, he reached into the folds of his shawl and pulled out my mobile phone, the one I'd unknowingly left at the ticket counter. Handing it to me, he said with a faint smile, "You're lost in your thoughts. Be careful with your belongings."

I stared at the phone, surprised, humbled by his quiet watchfulness. "Thank you, sir," I said sincerely. He returned my thanks with a smile, then, instead of walking away, he looked at my eyes, and he lowered himself onto the bench beside me.

There was a pause, heavy but not uncomfortable, and then he asked gently like a friendly neighborhood old man.

"This land is very special, my boy. What is yours will find you here, while what isn't will vanish. If they cannot find you, they will draw you to them. So, what have you lost? What are you seeking?" he asked, breaking the silence, with the tone of a kind old neighbor.

A few days ago…

Lord Kalabhairava sat silently, his expression revealing a deep concern as he read the message from Kaashi Vishwanath. He said gently to Nandi, "This request is extremely difficult. It doesn't seem possible in the way it's presented."

Lord Kalabhairava, the stern protector of time and fairness, was an amazing sight. He held a vessel of divine liquor in his left hand and a smoking pipe in his right. He was a very tall man, dressed in black clothes that were as dark as deep space. You could feel the raw, wild power coming off him.

When Nandi arrived bearing the command of Lord Kaashi Vishwanath, Kalabhairava's mood changed to one of wild excitement..

Nandi spoke in a warning tone, helping Kalabhairava grasp the complexity of the situation.

"Do you even realize who is making this request?"

Kalabhairava, still trying to make sense of it, replied, "Yes, I understand."

Nandi continued, his tone reflective and firm, "We must obey this as a command from the Lord. He has authority over this land and so the entire universe. In his grand scheme, we are merely small pieces of the puzzle. If he chooses to look past us, we may feel insignificant."

As Kalabhairava pondered the implications of Kaashi Vishwanath's words, he asked, "Where is he?"

When I woke up, it was still dark, but my heart was hammering. The air felt thick, heavy with the leftover feeling of a dream I could not quite remember. I looked around, my eyes trying to make sense of the faint shapes in my room. Shadows gathered in the corners, and a thin line of moonlight sneaked through the window.

My throat was dry, and a quiet sense of panic was bubbling in my mind. I reached for the glass of water on my nightstand. The cool water helped calm me as I drank, each gulp pulling me back to the real world. I took a slow breath, leaned back into my pillow, and tried to let sleep take over again.

At first, I thought it was just a random dream, a strange trick my mind played on me during a restless night. But then it came back, night after night, each time clearer than before. The images were hard to pin down, but they felt heavy, like whispers I couldn't quite understand. Day by day, my dreams started to scare me. Their weight pressed down harder, stirring up a restless feeling I just couldn't shake.

For days, that word "Kaashi" had haunted me. No matter where I went, whether in the woods or underwater caves, either the sounds or the formations, everything from nature seemed to urge: Go to Kaashi.

They were not just dreams anymore. They were a **call**. A purpose that seemed to be pulling me towards something I did not yet understand. From that moment on, the haunting began, with one name burning in my mind: **Kaashi**. It was a mystery, a pulse echoing in my veins, demanding that I chase it, no matter where it led. The calling grew so strong, it made me give up my job to search for it.

The next morning, the dreams were still fresh in my mind as I got ready for work. The usual traffic felt heavier than usual on my way to the office, each honk and slow crawl only adding to the strange pull I felt. While my mind was trying to stitch the thoughts from the dreams to find out any clue from them about Kaashi, I finally got to my desk.

Time seemed to fly by as I was lost in all of this but suddenly remembered to focus on the most important thing, reconsideration of my job resignation, on what was supposed to be my last day. My manager and bosses offered me an extension, one more month, but only if I accept it right away.

I was thinking a lot about this and wondering about continuing with work so that I could get busy at work and be able to push away and ignore the callings and dreams I am getting about Kaashi. As I was about to reconsider, a thought whispered, clear and powerful: **Go, Kaashi.**

It filled me with a sudden but strong numbness and tranquillity. Amidst all this, my manager entered my office and asked, "What have you decided?"

"I am not interested in continuing here," I replied firmly. "Thank you for your concern, sir."

He was taken aback, but he accepted my choice and asked me to complete the formalities for checkout. I agreed.

He believed I would reconsider, knowing how crucial the job was for me, especially given my financial situation and debt. It was true that without this job, I could not sustain myself. But I felt drained by work, by money, by emotions, and most of all… by life.

After taking care of all the paperwork, I listened to my gut feeling and decided to learn more about Kaashi. I had no clue what it was. I had never heard anyone talk about it, not in my neighborhood, not among my friends, and not even in the news. Just so you know, I am from North America and I live in Mexico.

At home, I asked my mother about Kaashi. She seemed unfamiliar and confused. After a moment, she looked at my father's portrait and said, "If your father were still alive, he would have told you about it."

I lost my father to cancer during childhood. After his death, my mother married her former lover, who was also a close relative. They have a daughter, Olivia.

My mother deeply grieved for my father but eventually accepted the fate. My stepfather promised to care for me, and she married him for support. She has always loved me deeply. My stepfather relies on me, and we share a respectful bond.

My amazing sister, Olivia, cares for me a lot. I am the most important person in her life, and she always has my back. As I grew older, I began earning to support the household. At times, I had to borrow money for basic needs.

My two best friends, Daniel and Carlos, were always there for me, helping me relax and forget my worries.

Daniel is a serious businessman who handles his family duties with ease and makes brave choices. **Carlos**, a mechanic, takes care of his parents and lives a happy, carefree life. Even though we come from different worlds, the three of us share a strong bond. We often get together, laughing, joking, and simply enjoying each other's company.

At one such meeting while we were hanging out at the bar, I asked both of them "That's all okay, but I want to ask you guys something..." and immediately Carlos replied, "Except for Kaashi, you can ask anything."

I asked him in shock, as I had not told them anything about my Kaashi hunt, "How did you find out about this?"

He retorted, "You have been talking about this endlessly. It seems your Kaashi obsession is all anyone's discussing in our area. I know you want to know more, but I don't have any information about it. Why are you so fixated on something which none of us around here seems to know about?"

I replied, filled with curiosity, "No, Carlos... It does not seem that simple. Recently, I had a magnificent dream in which I saw a place that is so divine on the banks of a river. That sight itself was so satisfying, and the next moment, I was on the streets, running as if a dog was chasing me. Even on the day I left my company, a saint covered in white powder with a snake idol on his head suddenly appeared, told me to go to Kaashi and vanished. All of this happened in a moment and is confusing me so much... It's like someone wants me to go there so desperately that they started haunting me"

Carlos seemed frightened after hearing this and said, "I think it must have been a bad dream or you must be just hallucinating, man. I know you are stressed about this but I do feel you must take care of your health."

Daniel asked, unaware of the subject, "Hey, what is Kaashi? Why are you both discussing something that is off-topic? Are you guys planning for a trip or something without me? You'll not celebrate your next birthdays" grinning and acting as an antagonist from old movies.

Carlos and I looked at each other and started laughing. Daniel was looking at us confused but started laughing with us after a few minutes. We started chatting about some other things and the topic deviated to more worldly matters. After spending a good amount of time together after so long, the three of us left for our homes.

As I settled into my bed, thoughts swirled in my mind, and I found myself shouting, "What is Kaashi? And where is it? It must be the name of the place from my dreams. I should find out by whatever means and should stop this haunting."

I began asking people throughout the city, my neighbours, friends, and even beggars on the streets. No one seemed to know its location. The mystery of this place was a silent question mark, pulling at my thoughts, leaving a knot of fascination in my stomach. Suddenly, I spotted my ex-lover, Elena.

After eight years, I found myself face-to-face with her again. When our eyes met, a polite, almost wary, smile touched her lips.

"Well, look who it is," she said, her gaze sweeping over me quickly. "What are you doing now?"

"Just resigned," I said, feeling a surge of unexpected lightness. "Heading to Kaashi."

Her carefully constructed politeness cracked. Her brows knitted slightly. "Kaashi? Is that... some kind of project or place? Where even is that?"

"I do not know," I admitted, the simple truth hanging in the air.

Her eyes scanned my face, the practiced calm in them fading into a sharp, familiar disappointment.

"So," she said, her voice heavy with resignation, "still wandering, aren't you? Always chasing something just out of reach." A bitter laugh escaped her lips. She continued, "That is the problem, isn't it? You do not even know what you are looking for, yet you expect the world to lay it at your feet." She leaned closer, her tone cutting despite its quiet. "Heaven help anyone who gets tangled up in your mess."

With a flourish, she pulled a magazine from her bag and thrust it toward me. "Look," she said, her gaze piercing. "My husband, see what he has built. That is real. That is what lasts." She paused, letting the weight of her words settle.

Elena spoke immediately "No need for it, Dear. Some of us move forward, try to do something and achieve in our lives. And there are others… Well, they just do not, like him."

As I glanced at the magazine, a spark flared in my mind of why had I not thought to search for Kaashi in the library? The realization hit like a burst of light, and a quiet thrill surged through me. I gave a faint nod, the word "Thanks" catching in my throat, hollow and unnecessary. Turning away, I hurried off, my steps quick with newfound purpose, eager to chase the answer now burning bright.

There's a unique moment in everyone's life when the world outside falls silent and a voice within whispers, **"Go find yourself."** For me, that was the same moment.

Since childhood, I had carried this persistent need to understand, not just the *what*, but the fundamental *why*. Superficial answers never settled my soul. If something did not feel right, my spirit would not rest until I had dug deeper and unearthed what truly mattered.

That inherent restlessness was still very much a part of me. Only now, it felt louder, more insistent.

I had been running a race I never signed up for, a race that rewarded surviving over living and experiencing life, a race where you are just expected to follow societal rules instead of finding your own path.

So, I decided to press pause on the life others or society want me to live. Not because I was tired or incapable (though I knew some perceived it that way), but because I was finally ready to listen to what I had been silencing, the questions I buried under deadlines, the emotions I postponed in the name of growth.

I was not trying to prove anything to anyone. At that moment, I felt truly free, without any shackles or tied-up chains. I was just turning inward, towards the child within me who still asked, "What is Kaashi? "

I summoned Carlos and Daniel to the city's central library, a cavernous place brimming with knowledge. If answers about Kaashi existed, they'd be here.

Carlos groaned as we arrived. "Seriously? This dusty old place? I was convinced it was cursed when I was a kid. And all for this... this obsession you have with Kaashi?"

Daniel shrugged. "Let's just give it a shot, Carlos."

We split up, combing through the dimly lit stacks. Carlos and Daniel tackled the geography section while I scoured history.

Carlos muttered, "If we had studied this hard in school, we would be scientists by now."

Daniel chuckled, but hours slipped by, yielding nothing. Then, tucked inside a heavy tome on world history, I found a folded sheet of paper. I pulled it out carefully and unfolded it across a table. It was a massive world map, its edges worn but legible.

"What's that?" Daniel asked, peering over.

"A map, specifically a pilgrimage world map" I said. "If Kaashi is a real place, it has to be on here."

The map was a maze of tiny names. I grabbed a magnifying glass, scanning for "Kaashi." Carlos and Daniel traced the map's edges, and I skimmed names, Mecca, Vatican city, Lumbini, and then… Kaashi.

"Daniel, here!" I shouted, my pulse quickening.

"No way, it's real!" Daniel said, his voice bright with excitement.

Carlos squinted. "It's in India."

I quickly located a book specifically on Indian history, and what I discovered there took my breath away. Kaashi wasn't merely a location; it was a living, spiritual heart, considered eternal. People journeyed there seeking a life of devotion, often becoming sadhus. Its river, sacred and deeply revered, drew countless worshippers daily. Kaashi was understood to be an immortal land in the Universe, a **karma bhoomi**, pulsing with divine energy, widely known in modern times as Varanasi.

Then, two names leapt from the page: **Nandi** and **Kalabhairava**. They struck like lightning, vivid and haunting, the same figures from my dream, their presence sparking this relentless pull. I showed my friends an image of them. Two figures in the image were almost identical to the characters I saw in my dream: Kalabhairava sitting on a black dog holding a trident, a drum, a skull, and a serpent in four hands, while Nandi, with a bull head and well sculpted human body, stood beside him pleasantly holding a sword.

Though their forms were hazy in my memory, their names burned with clarity, as if they had been summoning me all along. Kaashi was not a fleeting dream, it was a call. It's eternal rhythm now thrumming in my veins, urging me to follow where it led.

Carlos leaned forward, his eyes glinting with curiosity. "So, you are planning to go to India, right?"

I nodded, my heart racing with the weight of the decision. "Yeah, I have to see it for myself."

Daniel frowned, crossing his arms. "Hold up, what about your mom? You know she is not exactly a fan of India. Have you thought this through?"

Carlos shot Daniel a look. "Why are you stressing him out?"

Turning to me, he grinned, his voice warm and encouraging. "Listen, buddy, I get it, going to India is a big deal, especially for you. But next week is *Día de Muertos*, our festival. It is the time when hearts are open, when we honor what matters most. Find a quiet moment during the celebrations, maybe when Aunty lights candles for the *ofrenda*. Tell her about your plan then. She will feel the sincerity in your heart and will definitely agree."

I smiled, bolstered by Carlos's words, though a flicker of doubt lingered. Kaashi's call was undeniable, but the path ahead felt like a pilgrimage in itself, one that would test my resolve before I even set foot on its sacred soil.

The day had arrived, cloaked in the vibrant hum of *Día de Muertos*. Outside, our neighborhood pulsed with the glow of marigolds and flickering candles, families honoring the departed with *ofrendas* adorned with sugar skulls and *pan de muerto*. But inside our home, a quieter reverence held sway. My mother was in her meditation room, a sanctuary she retreated to on every full moon and new moon, a ritual as steady as the tides.

I stood at the threshold, my heart pounding with the weight of what I was about to say. Kaashi's call burned within me, but the thought of my mother's disapproval, a woman whose faith anchored our family, made my steps falter.

The room was dim, lit only by a single oil lamp that cast dancing shadows on the walls. At its center stood a sacred relic, a cylindrical stone, smooth and dark, its surface gleaming as if polished by the hands of time itself. It was no ordinary object; it had been passed down through countless generations, my mother often said, carried across millennia by our ancestors.

Its form was both simple and profound, a rounded pillar rising from a broad base, etched with faint, ancient markings that seemed to pulse with a life of their own. She called it the heart of our lineage, a bridge to the divine, and on sacred nights, she poured water over it, the droplets catching the lamplight like tiny stars before pooling in the stone's carved basin.

I had always thought this ritual was unique, as if our family alone on this earth communed with the eternal in such a way. The stone's presence filled the room with an unspoken power, as if it held the secrets of the cosmos, whispering to those who dared listen.

I stepped inside, the wooden floor creaking softly under my weight. My mother sat cross-legged before the stone, her eyes closed, her breath steady as a river's flow. Her face, framed by strands of silver-streaked hair, was serene, yet carried the strength of someone who had weathered life's storms through faith. The air smelled of sandalwood and the faint sweetness of marigolds from the festival outside, blending the sacred with the festive.

As I knelt beside her, her eyes fluttered open, sharp and knowing, piercing through the dimness like a beacon.

"What's the news, my child?" she asked, her voice calm but laced with a quiet authority that made my throat tighten.

I hesitated, the Kaashi image from the map flashing in my mind. I swallowed the truth, choosing a lie.

"I... I got a job offer. In Canada. I'm thinking of going there. For work."

The words hung heavy. The stone seemed to hum faintly, as if it sensed the deception. My mother's gaze narrowed, her lips pressed into a thin line. She tilted her head, eyes boring into me.

"Hmmm."

The sound I am always scared to listen to. It is a riddle, neither approval nor dismissal. I shifted uncomfortably, waiting for more, but she closed her eyes, returning to her meditation. The lamp flickered, casting shadows that danced across the stone.

"So... I'll let you know the details later?"

She remained silent, her face serene but impenetrable. I rose, heart racing, and slipped out, the weight of my lie pressing on me.

I applied for a visa and went through a tough interview to finally get it. Given my financial situation, I could not afford anything I was doing until now, so my friends arranged everything for me, from the visa application to buying necessities, including flight tickets.

After somehow arranging some funds from my savings, I quickly packed my bag with only two pairs of clothes, keeping it minimal. I walked along the roads to the airport, which was close to my home, trying to articulate my feelings towards Kaashi, which grew quite difficult day by day. After successfully checking in, I boarded the flight, haunted by an unfamiliar emotion, with tears and happiness intertwined.

From the moment I stepped onto the soil of Delhi, India's vibrant capital, a tide of wonder crashed over me. The air pulsed with life, rickshaws jerked and wove through streets thick with people, vendors' calls cut through the din from behind steaming chai pots, the faint chime of temple bells drifted like blessings above the chaos. Ancient domes of mosques blazed in the sunlight, their marble scored with centuries of devotion, while saffron-robed sadhus glided like specters through the throng, their eyes ablaze with secrets.

The scent of jasmine, sharp and sweet, braided with the dry smell of dust and the rich warmth of spices, cumin, turmeric, something else I couldn't name, wrapped me in an embrace that felt both foreign and achingly familiar. This was a land of obedience and respect, its heritage etched not just in stone, but in every hand gesture, every bowed head.

I surrendered to India then, my heart swelling with gratitude for the choice I'd made to come, to answer the call that had haunted me since I first glimpsed Kaashi's name on a flickering screen.

Trains to Varanasi were unavailable, so I booked a bus, a 14-hour odyssey carving its way through the heart of India. The terminal was a barrage of color and noise, buses hunched, metal skins groaning under the weight of luggage; vendors barked prices over pyramids of samosas and glittering, garlanded idols; passengers shouldered past, their sacks of rice and battered suitcases dragging trails through the dust.

I boarded a crowded bus, compressing myself into a narrow window seat beside an old woman whose prayer beads clicked a dry, ceaseless rhythm, her lips a faint, focused motion of silent devotion. The air hung thick, a stale, humid wall of sweat, the sharp bite of turmeric, and the fumes of diesel, the cracked plastic seats groaning and gripping as the driver roared final checks and the engine caught with a shuddering roar. Discomfort seeped into every joint, elbows prodded mine, the loose window slapped against its frame, the heat was a heavy, smothering cloak, but none of it dulled the flame in my heart. kaashi was waiting.

As the bus heaved onto the highway, I braced my forehead against the cool glass, watching the city lights dissolve into smeared trails against the deepening twilight. Roadside dhabas punctured the passing darkness, their single lanterns casting shaky golden pools where truck drivers slumped over chai cups. A temple's silhouette etched itself against the bruised sky, its spire spearing the horizon like a silent prayer. I could not help but catalogue this to myself, a story writing itself onto the jolting ride. This was not just a ride; it was a pilgrimage, a thread fused to my very being. India's pulse beat a relentless rhythm around me in the dry click of the old woman's beads, the sudden, sharp cries at hurried stops, the distant, sweet smell of incense drifting on the night air. Every mile beckoned, that truth shining brighter than the ache in my cramped legs, the constant crush of strangers' shoulders, the slow, deliberate crawl of 14 hours.

In the morning, the bus cleaner shouts, "Kaashi, Kaashi, Kaashi." I get up and grab my backpack, but my excitement makes me impatient to put on my shoes, so I carry them in my hands. As I stepped into that sacred place, my legs felt newly energized.

I drifted through the streets, the distinct culture of the locals swirling around me in vibrant fragments – the flash of a saffron sari, the rhythmic clang of a street vendor's hammer, the intricate symbols chalked onto doorways. Kaashi wasn't just a city; it lived and breathed a living hymn, every corner vibrating with the divine.

I threaded my way through its ancient, labyrinthine streets, my senses inundated by the city's sacred rhythm – temple bells pealing from unseen temples tucked in shadowed alleys, the sharp, clean scent of camphor braiding with the sweet, thick perfume of jasmine on the humid air, the soft, steady chant of mantras swelling from the Ganga's ghats like an insistent tide.

The stones beneath my feet, worn smooth as river glass by centuries of devotion, felt warm, seemed to thrum with a deep, quiet power, as if kaashi itself held me in its ancient pulse. I'd come seeking a truth I couldn't name, but as I turned a corner, I collided with something that stopped my heart – a discovery that anchored me to this land in ways I'd never imagined.

Beneath the gnarled branches of a banyan tree stood a small shrine, its stone heart gleaming with water and adorned with marigold petals. The stone was smooth, cylindrical, rising from a carved base, its surface etched with faint markings that shimmered in the sunlight. My breath hitched, a tremor of recognition coursing through me. It was the same as the stone in my home, the ancient relic my family had tended for generations, its presence a constant in my mother's meditation room, anointed with water on sacred nights. I'd thought it was ours alone, a singular ritual that marked us as unique on this earth, a private offering to the divine. But here, in kaashi, it was not one stone but countless.

I moved through the streets, my eyes now wide, seeking and finding them everywhere. In temple courtyards, they stood draped with crimson cloth, smeared with sandalwood paste, surrounded by priests whose chants wove a tapestry of devotion. In roadside alcoves, they glowed under flickering oil lamps, tended by devotees who bowed with folded hands, their lips moving in silent prayer.

Even children clutched small replicas, their laughter mingling with the city's sacred hum as they darted through the crowds. Each stone was a twin to the one I had known, its form a silent anthem that echoed through kaashi's soul. My family's ritual, which I had held as ours alone, was woven into the very fabric of this eternal city.

I paused at a temple, its doorway framed with jasmine garlands, where a sadhu with ash-smeared skin poured milk over another stone, the liquid pooling in its base like an offering to eternity. A woman in a saffron sari knelt beside him, her voice a soft hymn, and I caught her words, clear and resonant: "Clear the space for everyone to see Shiva Linga" and every one spell the relic, "Om Namah Shivaya"

The name struck me like a bell, its syllables reverberating through my bones. Goosebumps pricked my skin, a shiver of awe and peace washing over me, as if the air itself had whispered a secret. My heart stilled, then swelled, a tide of emotions I couldn't name, reverence, belonging, a quiet joy that felt like coming home. Om Namah Shivaya. The words carried a weight I had never known, a truth that linked the stone in my home to every shrine in kaashi, to every prayer rising from this sacred land.

The sadhu's eyes met mine, and he smiled, as if sensing my wonder. "Om Namah Shivaya," he repeated, his voice low, and I felt it again, goosebumps, a warmth spreading through my chest, a peace so profound it silenced the chaos of the world. The name was a mantra, a key to the divine, and hearing it here, in kaashi, was like hearing my own soul spoken aloud.

I stood rooted, watching the stone's surface pulse with a light I could feel but not see, its carvings alive with the same power I had sensed in my family's relic. This was no mere object, but a bridge to the eternal, a symbol of Shiva himself, whose presence I felt in the city's heartbeat, in the distant chant of "Hara Hara" drifting from the ghats.

I followed the signs pointing towards The Kaashi Vishwanath Temple and, along the way, spilled out onto Dashashwamedh Ghat. The place throbbed with energy, crowds churned and flowed, a river of humanity, individuals and families immersed in rituals, each face a study in devotion, lost in their own prayers and offerings, the sweet smoke of incense twisting, the soft splash of water offered to the Ganga, the flicker of countless small lamps set afloat.

I sank onto one of the ancient steps, drinking it all in, letting the sheer intensity of the moment engulf me. As my gaze scanned the vibrant scene, I caught the eyes of a few people. They held my gaze, their curiosity a palpable weight in their eyes, filled with silent questions.

I have a fair complexion, thick black hair, and a plump appearance. My eyes shine blue, and I have a round face with a clean-shaven look. I wore a single earring in my left ear, along with some crystal bracelets and a Rolex watch, a gift from my ex-lover, Elena.

I put on a brown jacket to prepare for the weather, although it felt quite sunny today. I wore jeans and sunglasses to shield my eyes from the bright sun. I continued to ask people about the Kaashi Vishwanath Temple and eventually found a long queue waiting for his darshan.

Suddenly, I spotted the same saint who once instructed me to come to Kaashi. My heart pounded as I called out to him, but he didn't stop. He moved quickly, his steps firm and confident. He carried a stick in one hand, his body bare, exuding an air of purpose.

Without hesitation, I pushed through the crowd, trying to keep up with him. But no matter how fast I moved, I could not match his speed. He weaved through the people effortlessly, while I struggled, my heavy backpack slowing me down.

At one point, I lost sight of him in the sea of devotees. Frustrated, I stopped and asked the people around me if they saw him. They pointed in a direction without speaking, just gesturing with their hands.

I followed their signs, and within seconds, I spotted him again. This time, I decided not to lose him.

Ignoring the weight on my shoulders, I picked up my pace, determined to find out why he wanted me here in the first place. He walked with unwavering speed, headed straight towards a Kalabhairava temple. As he approached, something strange happened, the dense crowd instinctively parted, making way for him. Without thinking, I followed suit.

He entered the Kalabhairava Temple, one of the most powerful and revered temples in Kaashi.

As he reached the deity, a group of saints gathered around him. They all looked identical, clad in the same ash-covered clothing and exuding the same intense aura.

Numerous individuals engaged in conversation with their neighbours, while some recited mantras dedicated to Kalabhairav. Meanwhile, I found myself eagerly anticipating his presence. I felt uncertain about the connection that draws me here, but something compelled me. As I drew closer to him, a saint blew a conch shell, and another saint played the Damaru.

One of the saints halted me and instructed, "Tell him I have arrived."

I asked him, shocked to the core, "Why?"

He insisted even more firmly, "Say, I have arrived."

I echoed his words, "I have arrived."

As soon as I spoke those words, the people around me began chanting Kalabhairava's mantras even louder, their voices rising to the point where it feels like their throats might give out. The energy in the temple grew intense, almost overwhelming.

Suddenly, one of the saints in the crowd shoved me forward. I lost my balance and stumbled straight into the temple's main door, falling towards Kalabhairava's idol. My hand landed on the deity's feet.

The moment I touched it, a strange force surged through my body. It felt like an electric shock gripped my hand. Startled, I pulled away immediately.

I looked down at my palm, it covered itself in a fine layer of white powder. A sharp pain spread through my hand, unlike anything I had felt before. My body tenses, and I could not stop myself from shouting in pain.

I stared at my hand, confused and terrified. Something happened to me, something I cannot understand.

Kala Bhairava appeared in front of Nandi. He seemed so confident like he accomplished an important job.

"As per the direction of Lord Kaashi Vishwanath," he said. His voice was deep and sounded final "I have brought him. What should we do now?"

Nandi sat quietly, looking like he had been there forever. He turned his big head. His deep eyes seemed to understand everything, maybe even a little bit like he found it interesting or wise. A slow, knowing smile spread across his large face.

"Just leave it to him," he said in a low voice. He sounded very sure about something that was going to happen next. He wasn't looking at Kala Bhairava, but out at something big and still happening far away.

Chapter 2

The Streets

My neck ached as I stepped down into the sun-drenched square outside the temple, the weight of my backpack dragging at my shoulders. The serenity of the inner sanctum had faded behind me, replaced by a sprawling chaos that buzzed with movement. I gathered my few belongings, now painfully aware of how little I carried, not just in weight, but in currency. I had to find a place to stay. Something cheap. Shared, if needed. Just a bed to rest my bones.

The streets ahead were narrow, winding, and seemed to care about nothing. They spread out like tangled threads in an old, worn-out prayer mat. When I had followed the Aghori through them, I had been too absorbed to pay attention. Now, the city felt like a puzzle missing half its pieces. I drifted through it, looking for a clue, a kind face, a sign.

Despite the growing heat and my mounting fatigue, strangely a piece of peace still wrapped itself around me like a shawl. My mind was unburdened, calm as if the storm within had gone silent, even as the city outside roared with life.

I asked the first few rickshaw drivers, street vendors, fruit sellers I passed but no one stopped. A shake of the head, a distracted wave, a muttered "Nahin pata." Kaashi never slows down for anyone. The city spins on its own axis, a riot of motion and sound. I felt like a half-seen, half-forgotten visitor in a dream.

The sound of a vendor flipping pakoras with his hardened bare hands in hot oil, the joy of children chasing the kites, the rhythmic repetition of "Chai, chai garam chai!" by a chai wallah - everything around me felt so alive and brushing against my weariness like a passing breeze.

I paused at a sweet stall where a wiry man molded golden laddoos with swift hands. The air around him buzzed with bees and the thick perfume of sugar. "Best in Kaashi, bhaiya!" he grinned, thrusting one toward me. I shook my head and asked, "Is there any place nearby bhaiya, to rest some time? At least a room?"

His grin dropped into a shrug. "All are full, sahib."

I moved on, scanning every corner for signs, "Clean Beds," "Cheap Stay," "Family Rooms", most were weathered and sun-bleached, some just painted words on broken boards. At a small guesthouse with a half-open door, I stepped in. A woman sat behind a counter fanning herself with a newspaper, her silver braid swinging like a pendulum with each motion.

"Excuse me, Any rooms available?" I asked, wiping the sweat from my temple.

She didn't even look up. "Not one, beta. All full."

"Any chance something opens soon?" I asked with a little bit of hope.

After a dry chuckle, She said, folding her paper, "In Kaashi, you wait. Let the plan unfold itself. I believe you should go and try near the ghats."

Though her tone was teasing and cryptic, It felt strangely comforting. I nodded and stepped back out into the street's river. I paused at a sugarcane cart. The vendor, darkened by sun and time, sliced long stalks and fed them into a creaking press. Juice trickled out into metal cups.

"Any vacant rooms you know of?" I asked, my voice almost lost to the crowd.

He handed me a cup, its rim sticky. "Drink first, bhaiya. No rooms now."

He winked and turned away. I stood still for a moment, the cold sugarcane juice sliding down my throat. The sun pressed down. The crowd moved around me. I had no bed, no map, no plan. But a voice from within was telling me confidently that something was waiting for me somewhere in this city.

I leaned against a cool wall, taking in the busy street. No guesthouse had rooms, but Kaashi still pulled me in. The sounds of carts, tea sellers, and a flute felt strangely comforting, making my heart beat with the city. A small hope sparked when I saw other travelers speaking Spanish, but they sadly told me there were no rooms anywhere, maybe in a week.

I would keep trying to find a place. But right now, just being lost in Kaashi's maze of streets was exactly where I wanted to be. It felt like home, even without a proper place to stay.

The wind shifted. A coolness swept through the street, and people instinctively tilted their heads skyward. The sky was eerily serene. Too serene as lightning flickered on the horizon like a whispered warning.

Far ahead, about a kilometre away, I spotted what looked like a vacant lodge. A flicker of determination sparked. I started toward it, but the streets resisted. Narrow lanes writhed with movement, motorbikes screaming past, their horns blaring like battle cries. My legs dragged, each step heavier than the last. Finally, I reached the spot.

Only it wasn't a lodge.

I stood at the edge of the Ganges, its wide, ancient current flowing before me. Confused, I spun around. The lodge was still in the distance. How? Had I missed it? Or was something twisting the streets beneath my feet?

I turned back, walked again, head down, steps slow. Fatigue blurred my vision. The alleys felt unfamiliar now, shifting as though the city itself was rearranging. Eventually, I arrived, again, at the riverbank. Same place. Same ghat. Same stretch of water staring back at me.

A sharp unease prickled my spine. I rubbed my eyes and looked again. The lodge still stood a kilometre away.

Yet when I turned again, the river was right in front of me.

Then, like an echo from a dream, the Aghori's words returned to me, words he'd spoken at the temple:

"You are planned and trapped here. You will be in a loop. Prepare for it."

The chill that gripped me then wasn't from the wind.

I sank down onto the stone steps of Varuna Ghat, my body folding into exhaustion. Draping a towel over my head, I sat in silence, staring at the river. I had nowhere else to go. Every road led me back here. The streets were toying with me, like a mischievous child tossing a pebble upstream just to watch it fall again.

Around me, life flowed on, untouched by my strange spiral. Women scrubbed clothes, their laughter ringing over the splash of water. Children shouted as they leapt into the river, diving for coins. A vendor roasted corn over a tiny flame, the smell curling into the air like smoke from a ritual. Nearby, men huddled over a game of cards, their voices rising and falling in a rhythm older than memory.

Kaashi didn't need to welcome me with open arms. She did it with these tiny, electric pulses of life. I let myself dissolve into the moment. For now, I belonged to this chaos.

Then came the buzz.

My phone vibrated in my pocket, and I pulled it out. The screen glowed with a name that made my chest tighten: *Ma*. Everything around me seemed to pause, the sparkle on the river's surface, the background hum of the ghat. My thumb hovered over the green button, but memory struck first, sharp and sudden.

That last night in the meditation room. The smell of marigolds thick in the air. The silence after my lie.

"I'll let you know the details later?" I had said, already turning away.

But she'd stopped me.

"I know where you're going," she'd said, voice quiet but unshakable. "Not Canada. I've seen that fire in your eyes. It's in your blood. If I try to stop you, you'll run, won't you? You'll go to that city no matter what I say."

I stood frozen, my lie undone in a single breath.

Her face had softened, but her resolve had not.

"If you must go to India," she'd said, "I have one condition. You return in ten days. And every day, you answer my call. Just tell me you're safe. If you can promise that, I'll let you go."

A strange mix of guilt and gratitude had bloomed in me then. I nodded, smiling faintly.

"Okay, Ma. I promise."

She had returned to her prayers, pouring water over a stone idol, the droplets falling like stars onto the floor.

Now, here I was, the river before me and her voice waiting behind the screen. I inhaled deeply, grounding myself in the ghat's hum, and answered.

"Ma?" I said, voice low.

She spoke, her voice laced with warmth and worry. "You're there, aren't you? In Kaashi?"

I nodded, though she couldn't see it.

"Yeah, Ma. I'm here. It's… it's incredible."

She sighed, relieved, but not fully.

"I'm safe. The city's alive, Ma. So much life, so much noise. I'm okay."

A sudden thought sparked, a way forward. *A boat.* If the streets circled me in a loop, maybe the river could carry me out. Maybe I could see Kaashi from a new vantage point, from the water that had watched centuries pass.

"Ma," I said, the idea taking shape, "I'm figuring out what's next. I'll call you tomorrow, okay?"

She agreed softly, her trust gently placed in my voice.

We hung up, the click quiet but final.

I looked out at the river again. The Ganga flowed on, steady and untamed. Somewhere down its length, stories waited, stories that might finally lead me out of the loop.

Or deeper into it.

A thought struck me, sudden, vivid: *Why not take a boat from here?*

The idea sparked like flint, simple, right. A chance to witness Kaashi from the river, to drift along the Ganga's winding course and see its soul unfold in ghats and silhouettes. It felt instinctive, like the river was calling me.

"Ma, I'm figuring things out," I told her, the thought still forming roots. "I'll call you tomorrow, okay?"

She agreed, her voice soft with a quiet trust. We said our goodbyes. The call ended with a gentle click.

The search began, frantic, hopeful. Every boat already packed, the oarsmen waving me off with tired smiles and helpless shrugs. The sun bore down, sweat collecting at my brow. The ghat buzzed with life, loud and relentless, but Kaashi's energy carried me, somehow.

Then, near the far edge where the crowd thinned and the river exhaled in soft ripples, I saw it. A small boat, old but sturdy, tied lazily to a post.

A lone boatman sat at its edge, mending a net, his face tanned and lined with time. I stepped closer, heart lifting.

"Can you show me all the ghats?" I asked.

He looked up. His eyes held stories.

"It's a private boat, sir," he said slowly. "One thousand rupees."

His voice was gravel and river water, rough, but calm.

I paused. Did the math. *Two thousand rupees... twenty dollars.*

"Okay," I murmured, the decision settling like a stone in still water.

I stepped in. The wooden planks creaked under my feet. Anticipation bubbled.

I sat on a narrow bench as the boatman untied the rope with practiced ease. The boat rocked gently, ready to give in to the current,

, when a figure emerged at the water's edge.

He moved with intent. Ash-covered skin, dreadlocks heavy with time and beads, a bundle in one hand. An Aghori. The ghat's noise seemed to hush around him.

The boatman turned to me, voice suddenly softer. "Sir, one small favour. Can we drop him on the other side? He's... one of the most powerful Aghoris here."

I looked at the man, chalky white against the city's vibrant chaos, and felt a flicker of curiosity, laced with unease.

The boatman added, "Please, sir. Why should we trouble them?"

I nodded. Hesitant. The Aghori was already beside me before the nod was even done. I shifted to the other side of the bench, giving him space.

We glided forward, the boatman pointing out each ghat, naming them, telling stories.

I watched people in the water, dipping, praying, whispering to the river.

"Does this happen only here?" I asked.

The boatman smiled. "This is India, sir. We thank even the air we breathe. We say sorry and thank you for everything."

Then I noticed her.

On a cement rooftop near a temple, a young female Aghori, deep in meditation.

She was draped in black, a dupatta over her shoulders, a black tilak shining on her forehead. People paused to worship her, leaving offerings at her feet.

She looked... ethereal. Her smile felt like it didn't belong to this world.

"Who is she?" I asked.

The boatman shot me a quick, irritated glance. "She came a few months ago. One of the most powerful Aghoris in Kaashi. Don't interfere with her, sir."

I looked away, just in time to catch smoke rising. Flames crackled.

"What's that?" I asked.

"That's Harishchandra Ghat," he replied. "The largest cremation ground in the world."

And then, the Aghori beside me spoke. Loud. Echoing.

"Every beginning will end here. And that end will become endless in the universe!"

His voice thundered. A chill ran down my spine.

He stood suddenly, raising his staff to the sky.

The clouds darkened. Wind whipped across the river.

With a crack, he slammed his staff against the boat's floor. Everything shook.

I lost balance,

, and fell.

The river swallowed me.

I surfaced once, gasping, then sank again.

"Help! Help!" I screamed, but the river roared louder.

I broke the surface, barely, reaching out, fingers brushing the boat's edge, before being pulled under again.

I thrashed. Reached blindly.

Caught the boat.

Clung on.

With one last surge, I hauled myself up and collapsed onto the deck, coughing, choking, drenched.

My body trembled. My mind reeled.

I turned to the boatman.

"Where is he?" I asked, between gasps.

"I dropped him off on the other side, sir," he said calmly. "You're lucky, sir."

"Lucky?" I asked, still shaking.

He laughed softly, almost in disbelief.

"Sir, you dipped three times in the middle of the Ganga. And lived."

His words barely sank in. I was still caught in the echoes of what had just happened. Still wet, still cold.

We reached Raja Ghat. I stumbled off the boat. My clothes clung to my skin.

I hadn't found a place to stay.

I kept walking.

Hours passed. My clothes dried on my back, but my energy drained. I finally found a lodge and asked for a room.

They asked for an advance.

I reached into my pocket,

Empty.

Wallet. Gone. Phone. Gone.

A cold wave of panic crashed over me.

My wallet had everything. My ID. My cards. My cash.

When did I last see it?

On the boat. When I paid him.

I stood there, frozen. Lost.

I walked back to Raja Ghat. Sat down on the steps. Nowhere else to go.

The night sky stretched above.

I lay back.

And fell asleep.

I was in a forest. Vast. Silent.

No one stirred. The trees towered above, shadows cloaking everything.

Only the moon watched.

In my hand, a fire stick flickered, my only light. It cast jagged shadows as I walked forward, unsure where or why.

Something called to me. Not in words. But deep, inside.

Each step echoed loud against the hush. Then,

A sound. A low, vibrating hum.

"Om."

It rose from the earth, from the trees, from within.

I stopped.

Then followed it.

My fire stick trembled in my grip.

A shimmer above, a cobra moved along a branch. Its scales glinted like oil.

My heart pounded, but I kept walking. The hum led me deeper.

Into something I still didn't understand.

Then came another sound, footsteps, rapid and heavy, someone running through the forest. I could sense them, their rhythm slicing through the hum of the "Om," but I saw no one. My chest tightened. The fire stick's warmth pressed against my palm as I quickened my pace. The trees parted suddenly, and I found myself at the edge of a hill, the ground dropped sharply into a vast, dark void. My foot slipped on loose soil. For a moment, I teetered on the brink, but I caught myself just in time, gripping an exposed root to steady my stance.

I looked around, breathless. The hill stood taller than all the rest, towering above a deep, endless forest. The full moon hung enormous in the sky, its light piercing through shifting clouds, painting the world in hues of silver and shadow. Across the chasm, I saw a cave, its dark mouth carved into the opposite hillside. It exuded power, ancient and commanding, as if it held secrets older than time itself. The scene around me felt surreal, like stepping into an adventurous film from my childhood. That same thrill of wonder and danger pulsed through my veins.

The fire stick in my hand flickered as I took in the vast view, the cave calling to me with silent power.

But then, a chill. I sensed something behind me, approaching too quickly. I turned too late. A force pushed me, deliberate and strong. I fell. The fire stick slipped from my grasp as the wind howled past me, the ground rushing closer.

Just as I was about to hit it, just as death seemed certain, I jolted awake.

My body sprang upright, breath ragged, skin drenched in sweat. I was on a ghat, sprawled across its cold stone steps. The Ganga murmured softly in the distance. The night air was cool. The moon still floated high above, casting silver trails across the river. I wiped the sweat from my face with my sleeve, heart slowly calming, the terror of the forest fading with each breath. It had been a dream, but it clung to me, heavy and vivid, as if I'd truly fallen.

I lay back down, letting the quiet of the ghat wrap around me, and slowly drifted back into sleep.

A few hours later...

Even in sleep, something stirred uneasily within me. A soft, rhythmic chanting of "Om" began to echo nearby. But instead of fear, I felt calm, soothed, as if held by something divine.

I opened my eyes slowly. The sun had risen, its golden light making me squint. Rubbing my eyes, I tried to focus. And there she was, the young woman I had seen before at Harishchandra Ghat.

She was meditating.

A strange peace washed over me as I watched her. Her presence felt like fresh air in a heavy world. Even in chants, her voice was gentle, melodic. Her long, curly hair framed a face that glowed with quiet divinity, like she didn't quite belong to this world.

Just as she began to open her eyes, I quickly shut mine, pretending to sleep.

Moments passed. I peeked through slitted eyelids. The sunlight bathed her in gold. And then, I noticed something beside me, my wallet and phone.

As I fully opened my eyes, she gently leaned back and looked at me. Without a word, she handed over my belongings.

A wave of relief and gratitude surged through me. My voice escaped before I could think: "Hi."

But she didn't stay.

She simply turned and walked away, melting into the crowd. Just before she disappeared, she glanced back, just once.

And then she was gone.

Far away, in the region of Mount Kailash, beyond Rakshastal Lake...

Sixty-four thousand seven hundred thirty-two demons stood sentinel, guarding the sacred path that led into the mountain. Among them, three stepped forward, Vikata, Karkataka, and Krura. Their forms were monstrous, terrifying.

Their clothes were tattered hides of fresh animal skin. Sharp, jagged teeth jutted from their mouths. Around their wrists and ankles clinked bracelets made from human teeth, souvenirs from those they had slaughtered. Blood had long since dried on their thick, dark skin. Their eyes gleamed with a cruel brown glow. Their noses were flat, mere holes above lips that curled with hunger. Their tongues, razor-sharp, could kill with a single bite. Thick, matted hair clung to their scalps like twisted vines. The stench of rot clung to them. They wielded massive weapons made from animal bones, stained deep with blood. With each step, the earth seemed to recoil.

They stood in the icy barrens, surrounded by snow-capped peaks, frozen lakes, and shadowy valleys. The temperature had plunged to -40°C, the air sharp and unforgiving.

These three were not just any demons, they were legends of terror. In the horrific realm of Patalaloka, none were feared more than Vikata, Karkataka, and Krura. Their names were curses, whispered only in dread.

Vikata, the embodiment of rage, was a monstrous fusion of molten stone and cursed iron. His roar could collapse mountains. His fists had crumbled entire planets. He delighted in tearing enemies limb from limb, soaking himself in their blood.

Karkataka, the strategist, was as cruel as he was calculating. With a scorpion-like form clad in void-black armor, he struck with silent precision. He played with his prey, weaving despair before delivering a fatal blow.

Krura, the sadist, had a skeletal frame pulsing with necrotic energy. His laughter was a chorus of pain. A single touch could reduce flesh to ash. He twisted his victims' agony into grotesque art.

And above them stood their master: **Sukracharya**, the revered guru of Patalaloka's demons.

Clad in robes woven from starlight stolen from dying galaxies, Sukracharya was a being of immense wisdom and fear. His single eye saw through time itself, burning with the intensity of a thousand suns. His voice echoed with the weight of cosmic truths.

His training was brutal. In his vast obsidian arena, demons were forged into weapons of destruction. He once made a student fight its own shadow for a century to master control. And from his teachings emerged warriors nearly invincible.

One day, he addressed them:

"You are forged to dominate. To crush. To burn through the threads of existence itself. But remember this, never challenge **Lord Vishnu**, **Lord Shiva**, or **Lord Brahma**. You may slay their warriors, but against them, even your might will crumble."

Among his disciples, **Karkataka** stood out. Brilliant, disciplined, and obsessed with mastery, he absorbed every lesson like a sponge of darkness. To Sukracharya, he was a reflection of himself, a being destined to surpass all others.

One cursed day, the trio tasted **dragon blood**, a forbidden nectar burning with primal power. Its essence drove them mad with ecstasy. From that moment, they became addicted. They began hunting dragons across the cosmos.

In every realm, dragons fought valiantly, but Vikata crushed skulls, Karkataka pierced hearts, and Krura drank deep from their wounds. The trio's cruelty was unmatched. Majestic creatures, symbols of eternal power, were reduced to broken husks.

The universe grieved. Stars dimmed. Galaxies mourned.

Their path was one of desecration, their thirst unquenchable.

In the divine realm of **Aadi Kagola**, where rivers shimmered with starlight and ancient forests thrummed with celestial life, the **Kimpurushas** reigned. These lion-headed titans, born from Brahma's sacred will, were guardians of balance. Their golden manes blazed, and their starfire blades could cut through galaxies.

Aadi Kagola was a haven of beauty and peace, until darkness arrived.

The demons of Patalaloka, led by the dreaded trio, Vikata, Karkataka, and Krura, had developed a ravenous addiction to dragon blood. In their own cursed realm, the blood of dragons was a bitter elixir, but in Aadi Kagola, it was ambrosia, intoxicating and divine. Driven by this insatiable craving, the demons descended upon Aadi Kagola like locusts, slaughtering its dragons with savage glee. They tore through scales, drank deeply of the crimson rivers, and left desecrated carcasses strewn across sacred groves. The once-vibrant forests wailed, and the stars dimmed in mourning.

When the Kimpurushas discovered the carnage, their hearts burned with grief and fury. "These fiends defile our home, our creatures, our very soul!" roared Rudravira, their mightiest warrior, his golden eyes blazing. "We will protect Aadi Kagola, no matter the cost!" The Kimpurushas, trillions strong, vowed to shield their universe from the demons' blasphemy.

One fateful day, the Kimpurushas ambushed a demon scouting party, trapping them in the crystalline canyons of Aadi Kagola. The captives, blood-drunk and defiant, were bound in chains of starfire. Rudravira towered over them, his voice a low growl. "Leave our realm, or face annihilation. This is your only warning."

Word of the ambush reached Vikata, Karkataka, and Krura. The trio's laughter echoed through Patalaloka's caverns, a sound that curdled the blood of even their own warriors. "They dare challenge us?" Vikata bellowed, smashing a boulder with his molten-stone fist. "We'll drown their precious universe in dragon blood!"

Karkataka's scorpion-like tail twitched with amusement. "Let them cower behind their warnings. Aadi Kagola will be our banquet hall."

Krura, his skeletal form glowing with necrotic glee, licked his lips. "Their dragons, their forests, their Kimpurushas, all will bleed for us. Summon the horde. We go to war."

The demons' taunts reached Aadi Kagola, their mockery a venomous barb. Enraged, the Kimpurushas accepted the challenge, their trillions-strong army assembling on the plains of Viraatha, a battlefield where the very ground pulsed with divine energy. The demons arrived in their millions, a writhing mass of bone blades, cursed armor, and bloodstained maws, their eyes glinting with hunger.

The war erupted with apocalyptic fury. The Kimpurushas charged, their roars shattering the heavens. Rudravira led the vanguard, his starfire blade cleaving through demons like a comet through the void. Each Kimpurusha was a force of nature, their blows toppling hundreds of foes. The demons fought with feral savagery, their bone-crafted weapons, curved scythes, jagged knives, and heavy cleavers, clashing against divine armor.

Vikata roared, his hammer crushing a Kimpurusha into golden dust. "Is this your strength, lionlings? You're prey, nothing more!" Karkataka darted through the fray, his venomous tail piercing Kimpurusha hearts, while Krura's necrotic touch reduced warriors to screaming ash. "Sing for me, divine ones!" he cackled, his laughter a blade of its own.

But the Kimpurushas were undaunted. Their blades flashed, and demons fell by the thousands, their bodies dissolving into Patalaloka's cursed essence. Yet, to the Kimpurushas' horror, something unnatural occurred. Each slain demon shuddered, split, and rose anew, three for every one struck down. The battlefield swelled with thrice the number of foes, their numbers growing like a plague.

Rudravira's eyes widened. "What sorcery is this?" he roared, cutting down a demon only to see it multiply before him. The Kimpurushas fought harder, their divine energy blazing, but the demons' numbers grew exponentially, a tide of darkness threatening to drown Aadi Kagola.

Amid the chaos, Karkataka paused, his cunning mind recalling Sukracharya's ancient training.

Karkataka, ever the attentive student, leaned forward, his claws twitching. Sukracharya's eye locked onto him, as if sensing his hunger for knowledge. "Fighting and killing divine soldiers is difficult," the master continued, "but you can drain their energy until their existence fades. Bleed their essence, trap it in our sieves, and their power becomes ours. Strike not to kill, but to exhaust. Let their divinity wither, and they will fall without rising."

A wicked grin spread across his face as he whispered to his brothers, "Our master taught us well. Fighting divine energies or their soldiers is futile, but we can drain their essence until their existence fades."

Vikata's laughter shook the ground. "Let's bleed them dry!" Krura's eyes gleamed with sadistic delight. "Their power will be ours to feast upon!"

The trio rallied their horde with a deafening cry. "Drain them!" they commanded. The demons shifted tactics, no longer seeking to kill but to exhaust. They swarmed the Kimpurushas, their bone blades grazing divine flesh, each strike siphoning slivers of their radiant energy. The Kimpurushas fought valiantly, but their strength waned. Trillions of lion-headed warriors, once invincible, felt their divine essence slipping away, trapped in the demons' insidious sieves, cursed artifacts that glowed with stolen power.

Rudravira, bloodied but unbowed, faced the trio. "You cannot destroy us!" he roared, his blade flashing. "Aadi Kagola will never fall!"

Karkataka's tail lashed out, grazing Rudravira's arm, drawing a pulse of golden energy. "Oh, we won't destroy you," he sneered. "We'll hollow you out, until you're nothing but echoes."

Krura cackled, his necrotic hand hovering over a fallen Kimpurusha. "Your dragons, your forests, your souls, all will feed us!"

Vikata loomed over Rudravira, his hammer raised. "Kneel, lion, or watch your universe choke on its own blood!"

The Kimpurushas, drained and dwindling, fought on, but the demons' laughter rang louder, a harbinger of Aadi Kagola's looming doom. The war was no longer a battle of blades but a theft of divinity itself, with the trio's cruel strategy turning the tide. The plains of Viraatha, once sacred, now wept under the weight of a trillion fading lights. Yet, they fell before the demon trio. The war spanned a thousand of years ago, a cataclysm that scarred entire dimensions.

Present...

Under the looming shadow of Mount Kailash, the sacred abode of Lord Shiva, the air thrummed with tension. The demon trio, Vikata, Karkataka, and Krura, had arrived from the abyssal depths of Patalaloka, following Sukracharya's cryptic instructions. Their mission was shrouded in mystery, a search for something unspoken, yet their presence desecrated the sanctity of the divine mountain.

Vikata, his molten-stone form casting jagged shadows, barked at his warriors, "Move forward!" His voice was a thunderclap, urging his men to scour the rocky slopes with relentless fervor. Krura, ever the sadist, trained his team with meticulous cruelty, his skeletal frame glowing faintly with necrotic energy. "Search every part of this place. Do not miss anything," he hissed, his words laced with menace as his warriors fanned out, their bone-crafted weapons glinting under the fading light.

Karkataka, however, stood apart, his scorpion-like form still as he gazed at Mount Kailash. His heart, though forged in Patalaloka's darkness, pulsed with reverence for Lord Shiva, the supreme divine power he held above all. Bowing his head, he offered silent prayers, his loyalty to the cosmic destroyer unwavering, even amidst his demonic kin.

A sudden rustle broke the tension. A messenger, trembling under the trio's gaze, delivered a letter sealed with Sukracharya's sigil. Krura's bony fingers tore it open, his dark eyes scanning the words. "Our master, Sukracharya, has called us back," he announced, his voice sharp. "He has decided to continue the search another day."

Vikata's massive frame quaked with fury. "What? We have already reached our destination! We are so close to finding the way!" he roared, his fists splintering a nearby boulder. His rage was a wildfire, untamed and defiant of their master's command.

Karkataka, still fixed on Kailash's snow-capped peak, spoke with eerie calm. "We will keep moving forward. Our supreme power will guide us." His words carried the weight of unshakable faith, a rare defiance rooted in his devotion to Shiva.

Krura's eyes narrowed, his voice dropping to a dangerous whisper. "Listen," he warned, "even the divine follows our master's orders. For us, God is and should be second to Sukracharya. We cannot go against his command."

Karkataka's laughter echoed through the valley, sharp and defiant. "Even our master draws his power from this supreme force. We trust the divine, not just his words." His conviction burned, a beacon of rebellion against Sukracharya's iron rule.

Yet, despite his fervor, Karkataka was outnumbered. Vikata's stubbornness and Krura's loyalty to their master prevailed. Reluctantly, Karkataka conceded, and the trio rallied their top warriors. "Search carefully. Do not miss anything," they commanded, their voices a chorus of dread. The warriors, armed with weapons hewn from animal bones, curved blades, razor-sharp knives, and heavy cleavers capable of shattering stone, spread across the mountain like a plague.

These weapons were no mere tools; they were extensions of the demons' cruelty. Forged in Patalaloka's infernal forges, some blades were long and wickedly curved, others compact but brutally efficient. A single strike could reduce boulders to dust, and many demons carried arsenals of smaller bone knives, perfect for carving flesh with surgical precision.

As the sun dipped below the horizon, darkness cloaked Mount Kailash. The demons returned to their makeshift camp, their grotesque forms settling into an uneasy rest. Some stood guard, their eyes glinting in the moonlight, while others groaned in their sleep, haunted by the weight of their sins. Husky voices murmured plans for the next day's search, and a few demons sat apart, tearing into the raw flesh of slain beasts, their lips stained with the blood of their prey. The air reeked of death and dragon blood, their favored elixir, which they drank with savage reverence. Eventually, exhaustion claimed them, and the camp fell into a deep, unnatural silence.

At dawn, as the first rays of sunlight kissed Kailash's peaks, a faint clattering stirred the camp, like nuts colliding in the wind. A demon guard, roused from his slumber, ignored the sound at first, grumbling in irritation. But the noise grew louder, more insistent, until it pierced his restless dreams. Frustration turned to dread as he opened his eyes, and froze.

Before him stood an Aghori, a figure of primal terror. His skin was pale as death, smeared with ash and filth, his knee-length hair a tangled mass of dirt and decay. Dark, hollow eyes burned with an otherworldly intensity, and his body was adorned with countless Rudraksha bead necklaces, draped across his chest and limbs like sacred chains. The air around him pulsed with an ancient, untamed power, as if the mountain itself had birthed him to guard its sanctity.

For the first time in his wretched existence, the demon felt fear, raw, paralyzing fear. The Aghori's presence was a silent proclamation: Mount Kailash would not yield its secrets to those who defiled its holiness. The demon's bone blade trembled in his grip, useless against the divine wrath incarnate before him.

Chapter 3

The Aghori

The demon's heart thundered. He leapt back, a full furlong, eyes wide with shock.

The moment he opened his eyes and saw the Aghori face-to-face, terror struck him like lightning. He froze, voice stuck, throat dry, eyes bulging as if about to burst. And then the Aghori stood up.

Behind him, an ocean of Aghoris rose.

It looked like death itself had arrived. The sight was so terrifying that the demon, still reeling, screamed, waking the others.

The horde of demons stared in fear. Though the Aghoris were far fewer in number, their presence was immense. Their bodies were smeared in white ash. Rudraksha beads weighed down their necks. Clad in nothing but sanctity, their hair coiled in wild knots, wrists and ankles adorned with Rudraksha bracelets, they stood like the wrath of time itself. Only eleven thousand strong, but overwhelming.

Vikata, Karkataka, and Krura stepped forward, attempting to understand the purpose of this dread march. One Aghori stepped out and warned:

"Leave this place. Now."

Vikata and Krura prepared to respond, but Karkataka surged ahead, defiant. He unleashed a thunderous war cry that shook the trees, sending snow crashing from their branches.

Demons roared in response, advancing in a frenzy. The ground trembled.

The Aghoris, their eyes blazing, marched forward with chants of **"Hara Hara Mahadev!"** Their voices cracked the sky. And in a heartbeat, the silent snowscape became a battlefield, a divine storm of ash and blood.

The battle began.

Each Aghori fought like an avatar of fury, bare-handed, yet unstoppable. One swing of a fist hurled demons into mountains. Another punch shattered the stone. One Aghori drove his fingers into a demon's chest and pulled out its heart. Another faced ten at once and dropped them all in a cascade of death.

Despite having no weapons, the Aghoris were unrelenting. No blow could stop them. No weapon could pierce them.

Vikata and Krura, master strategists of the demon army, watched in horror. Their plans failed. Their numbers faltered. Not a single Aghori had fallen.

Karkataka, enraged, tore through the planning setup and charged into battle. He slashed wildly, fists swinging in fury. But it was futile. Nothing landed. Nothing worked.

"Fall, zealots!" he screamed.

An Aghori sidestepped and vanished in a swirl of ash, only to reappear behind him and slice off Karkataka's claw with a sanctified blade.

"Your tricks are dust," the Aghori whispered.

Krura hurled spears laced with necrotic curses. **"Burn, fanatics!"** he shrieked.

But the curses dissolved on contact, nullified by divine chants and sacred ash.

Then the demons' hidden curse revealed itself: **every slain demon split into three.**

With every death, their numbers multiplied.

Vikata laughed, his voice manic.

"You cannot kill us. We are legion!"

Karkataka's eyes gleamed.

"Your Shiva will choke on our endless horde."

Krura cackled,

"Your light will drown in our darkness!"

The Aghoris, momentarily stunned, saw their foe multiply beyond reason. Even divine might seemed threatened. But we gave way to fury.

They lifted their heads, eyes burning with Shiva's fire. Their chants erupted:

"HARA HARA MAHADEV!"

Each syllable is a thunderbolt. Mountains cracked. Shadows dimmed. The sky trembled.

And then the **Aghoris feasted.**

Not on flesh, but on **existence.** They consumed demons entirely, name, memory, soul, vanishing them from the cosmos. Their hunger grew with every bite. The tripling curse turned on itself.

Demons kept multiplying. Aghoris kept devouring.

The tide turned.

Vikata's commands faltered. Krura's curses faded. Karkataka's fists slowed. Their laughter died.

An Aghori lifted a demon, spun it like a wheel, and slammed it headfirst into the earth, again and again, until nothing remained. Another Aghori grabbed a charging demon's arms and forced him to stab himself. A third crossed the demon's own knives into its neck, killing it instantly.

The chants rose louder. The air surged with divine energy. The mountains echoed the holy war cry.

"HARA HARA MAHADEV!"

From a force of death, the demon army shrunk, to just four thousand.

Vikata tried to rally the remnants, but an Aghori struck him down. His arms were torn from his body and thrown like red paint across the sky. His scalp ripped away, brain exposed. His eyes popped. Blood gushed like a fountain. The Aghori tore out Vikata's spine, and wore it as a garland. Then he picked up Vikata's severed legs and smashed down other demons with them.

Krura stood frozen, body trembling. He couldn't move. He couldn't blink. Shell-shocked.

Karkataka still fought, but his blows did nothing. The story would not change.

A final demon, trembling and broken, fell at the Aghori's feet.

"Mercy, lord of ash," it begged.

The Aghori loomed above, dreadlocks swaying.

His voice was soft.

"Shiva's hunger spares no profane."

With a single bite, the demon vanished, its existence undone.

Karkataka staggered back, his eyes wide with a flicker of memory. He recalled a distant war, in another universe, where they had trapped the Kimpurushas. The demons had drained their energy, believing victory assured. But the Kimpurushas' essence had surged with Lord Narasimha's primal fury, a force unmatched by any universe. It had roared with a ferocity that shattered the cosmos, its power overwhelming the demons' multiplication. The Kimpurushas had kicked off every demon, their divine wrath forcing the horde to flee in terror, abandoning that universe to Narasimha's roar.

And now, **it was happening again.**

Karkataka's claws trembled as he murmured to himself, "We cannot match our multipleness with this divine energy forever." The Aghoris' power, like that of Narasimha, was a cosmic tide: unstoppable and eternal. His brothers' laughter had faded, their once-mighty horde now reduced to mere echoes.

Desperation surged in Karkataka's voice as he shouted at Krura, forcing him onto the battlefield. Though fear gripped him to the core, Krura leapt forward and attacked an Aghori. But the Aghori calmly joined his palms, soared into the air, and delivered a crushing punch. Krura died instantly. The Aghori then sat atop his body, bending Krura's lower half over his own shoulder, making it seem like a grotesque swing.

Seeing this, Karkataka's resolve shattered. He turned to flee. But the Aghori who had slain Krura rose to his feet and began to dance, his movements fierce, echoing Shiva's tandav, as he swung Krura's corpse through the air, shouting praises to Lord Shiva.

Ten other Aghoris, scattered across the battlefield, witnessed the dance and joined in spirit. Spotting Karkataka as he ran, they moved in formation and chased him down. Surrounding him in a tight circle, they attacked together, ruthless and precise.

One by one, the demons fell, their lifeless bodies strewn across the blood-soaked ground. Each Aghori sat upon the fallen, tearing through their flesh without mercy. The few demons still gasping for breath were hunted down and slaughtered with the same brutal efficiency.

As the sun dipped toward the horizon, an Aghori grabbed a demon, slammed its head into the earth, and crushed it underfoot, marking the grim conclusion of the battle.

It had been six days since I began searching every ghat and street for her, but she was nowhere to be found.

Though I had a room, I chose to sleep on the streets, afraid that if I stayed inside, I might miss her. Every day, I wandered from temple to temple, road to road, learning something new in this sacred city of Kaashi. Each morning, I took a dip in the holy Ganga, letting her wash away the burdens and sins I had carried, both knowingly and unknowingly. But the darshan of Kaashi Vishwanath is occasionally disrupted due to overcrowding or other distracting circumstances. And I heard from some people around me that the darshan of kaashi vishwanath is not so simple and depends on what's destined for us.

Unlike any city I've ever known, Kaashi holds a mirror to the soul, reflecting its fragility as well as its boundlessness. Here, the line between man and beast blurs. I often shared my scraps of food with the dogs and cows that wandered the streets. As we ate, their eyes met mine, and in those moments, we were the same, two hungry beings, bound by the same pulse of survival. They took what was offered. I earned what I could. But in the eyes of the universe, there was no difference between us.

Today, hunger gnawed at me, a relentless ache that drowned out even the sacred chants echoing across the city. I yearned for something different, something that would taste of Kaashi's native soul. Rising from the worn mat in my cramped room above a chai stall, I reached for my purse, its leather cracked from years of travel. Inside lay a pitiful handful of coins, barely enough to survive the coming days or the journey that awaited.

I pocketed a portion of it and stepped into Kaashi's labyrinth of lanes. The streets throbbed with life: vendors shouting over sizzling tawas, sadhus chanting mantras, pilgrims moving toward the golden spire of the Kaashi Vishwanath Temple. The air brimmed with aromas, frying puris, spicy sabzis, crisp dosas on hot iron plates. My stomach twisted in longing for a simple, buttery slice of bread, a memory of home. But my coins offered no such luxury.

I stopped at a humble stall where an old vendor poured dosa batter with a practiced rhythm, timeless and serene. "One dosa," I said, my voice steady despite the hunger clawing inside. He nodded, and the tawa hissed. The scent of ghee and spice rose, a divine fragrance that silenced everything else.

When he handed me the dosa, crisp at the edges and steaming, I felt salvation within reach. But just then, a soft whimper interrupted me. I turned to see a street dog, its ribs pronounced, its fur matted, eyes hollow with hunger. It didn't beg, just waited, eyes locked with mine in silent hope.

My resolve melted. I tore the dosa in half and offered a piece. The dog took it gently, its gratitude aching in my chest. Then another dog appeared. And another. Each one silently asking, each one just as frail.

I gave them everything.

They ate ravenously, forming a quiet, trusting circle around me. When the dosa was gone, I used the rest of my coins to buy plain rotis with a smear of chutney. I fed them all, each bite a small offering to the sacred bond we shared.

I sat with them, my back against a temple wall, resting a hand on the head of the first dog. Its coat was coarse, but its warmth was a balm. My stomach remained empty, but my soul brimmed with peace. In this city where Shiva sees all, I felt the divine pulse that connects us, man and beast, hunger and grace.

Just as the last crumbs were licked from the ground, a shadow fell over me. I looked up to see a young boy, his clothes tattered, his face smudged with the dust of Kaashi. In his hands was a small offering, a roti folded with chutney. He extended it to me.

"For you," he said softly. "You fed them."

My throat tightened. "Why?" I asked.

He shrugged with a shy smile. "Because you did."

I accepted it, the warmth of the bread rekindling something deep within me. Above us, the temple's spire shimmered in the saffron dusk. Shiva was present, in the child's generosity, in the dogs' trust, in the rhythm of this ancient city.

Days passed. I kept searching. I returned again and again to the place where I had first seen the Aghori woman. Still, no sign. But the fire in my chest burned fiercer with each passing hour. I couldn't explain it. I only knew I had to find her.

That evening, I wandered to Dashashwamedh Ghat. The Ganga shimmered beneath the golden sky. Exhausted, I stood beneath the temple spire and whispered into the void, *"Shiva… please, let me see her again."*

As if in answer, the boy from before emerged through the crowd. His face was alight with urgency. "Brother," he said, breathless, "that Aghori told me to give the roti to you! She's there!"

He pointed toward a nearby temple.

My heart leapt.

There she was, ash-smeared, dreadlocked, adorned with Rudraksha beads, seated before a Shiva Linga, her lips moving in sacred chant. Her presence was unearthly, suspended between the mortal and the divine.

Our eyes met.

In that moment, the weight of my search, the hunger, the longing, everything, found its answer.

The priests poured white ash over the Linga and offered her a chance to do the same. She stepped forward and performed the ritual with grace. The ash drifted from her hands like a benediction.

Then, she turned and walked out.

I followed. The streets parted for her, vendors, pilgrims, all bowing in silent reverence. She entered an ashram, its carved doors marked with ancient symbols. I stopped outside, rooted to the earth.

The Ganga murmured behind me. Kaashi pulsed through my veins.

I waited.

Because in this sacred city of divine encounters, I was closer to her than ever before.

I wait through the night, body aching, mind alight with questions. I have no idea why I'm so drawn to her, but the need to speak with her burns like fire in my soul. At 3 AM, she emerges, calm, focused, walking toward the Kaashi Vishwanath Temple. I follow, her silence like a beacon in the pre-dawn stillness. She enters the temple with ease, unchallenged. I, however, am stopped at the gate.

After some time she steps outside, completed her worship, her rituals flowing like a silent hymn to Shiva. She leaves for the Panchganga Ghat, and I follow, steps heavy with fatigue. She begins meditating. I wait. But as hours pass, exhaustion takes hold, and I drift into sleep against the cool stones of the ghat. When I wake, dawn has painted the Ganges gold, and she is gone. I search in every direction, but she has vanished, like a specter lost in Kaashi's maze.

As part of my daily ritual, I take three dips in the Ganga. Its waters soothe my weary spirit. I returned to the ashram. For the next two days, I find her with surprising ease, almost as if Kaashi conspires to guide me. Sometimes, she appears just as my search falters, her presence both a mystery and a magnet. The curiosity to understand this synchronicity is second only to my desire to finally speak with her. I follow, waiting for a moment to bridge the silence.

On the ninth day, I called Carlos, a friend from my travels, to share what I've been experiencing in Kaashi. His voice crackles through the phone, warm and grounding.

"Take a break, brother," he says. "Don't stress yourself out. Go on that boat ride you mentioned. Enjoy Kaashi's magic."

Nervousness grips me. "No, no boat rides!" I replied sharply. "I had the worst experience."

"What happened?" he asks, curiosity sparked.

I recount the incident, words tumbling out. "When I took my first dip in the Ganga, a huge stone came rushing toward my face. I raised my hands to protect myself, palms open, and then something unbelievable happened. A golden energy formed between my fingers, like glowing strings. The rock, and others that followed, turned to ash. When I closed and reopened my hands, the power vanished, but when I tried again, it returned. I was shocked. I scrambled out of the water."

As I speak, the phone crackles, and then disconnects. My story is left suspended in Kaashi's mystic air.

I tried two more times to call back, but the line wouldn't connect. Frustrated, I turn, and there she is. The Aghori. Right in front of me. Her ash-smeared face holds a strange expression, as if she overheard everything. She nods, signaling me to sit on the stone steps of Scindia Ghat. We settle into the cool rock, the Ganges lapping beside us.

"Is that true?" she asks, her voice low and piercing.

"Yes," I nod, heart racing under her gaze.

"What happened next?" she presses.

Swallowing hard, I recount the second dip. "After surfing, I saw the Aghori who brought me there raise his stick to the sky and spin it in circles. Suddenly, all nine planets aligned in sequence. He grabbed them and hurled them into the river. I panicked and ran for the boat, but missed, and fell back into the Ganga. I saw the planets floating in the water. I was frozen. Then, the sun started moving toward me, as if it was about to strike. Out of fear, I opened my hands, and the planets, and that golden power, vanished. I rushed out, terrified." My voice trembles, my body shakes, as if reliving it. "I know I sounded like a coward. And honestly... I was. I still am."

"Then?" she asks, unflinching.

"The third dip was horrible," I whisper, the memory catching in my throat. "I couldn't even speak of it."

"Why? What did you see?" she asks, her curiosity intensifying.

"I saw a woman. Her body was black, thick, with smoke or fumes rising from it. Her hair was unimaginably long, flowing with the current. When she opened her eyes and stuck out her tongue, I screamed and ran out of the river." My voice shakes. Her eyes widen, face unreadable, as if absorbing the weight of what I've said.

"Since that moment... the power hasn't returned," I add, frustration creeping into my tone. I open and close my hands again, desperate, but nothing happens. A deep disappointment sets in.

She falls silent, as if lost in thought. I softly call her name. No response. Gathering courage, I gently touch her shoulder. She flinches, then turns to me.

"That power will return," she says calmly, "but only when you find and understand your true purpose."

Before I can ask more, she rises abruptly and walks away. Stunned by her words, I whisper, "When will we meet again?"

She pauses, turns slightly. "Like before, come to the ashram if you wish to see me. But don't wait outside, as you did these past few days." And with that, she walks off, her figure dissolving into Kaashi's golden morning.

I stand frozen. Shocked, she knew I had followed and waited. Back in my room, my mind races.

"What is my purpose?" I wonder.

"Is it to take power from Kalabhairava and return it to the river? Is that why I came? Is that why I lost the power?"

A strange pride rises. "What a great human I am," I tell myself, "transferring divine power from a temple to a river!"

I decide, *Tomorrow, I'll tell Carlos what I've done, he'll be amazed.* Slowly, I fall asleep.

It is my ninth night in Kaashi.

The next morning, I take my three dips in the Ganga, complete my rituals, and head to the ashram. As I arrive, she steps out, calm, as always.

"What are your plans today?" she asks gently.

"I'm leaving," I say, smiling. "I've fulfilled my purpose, just as you said yesterday. I'm happy with what I've done."

She nods, listening.

"But before I leave," I add, "I want to ask something."

"What is it?"

"I want to spend the day with you. Just today. May I?" My tone is almost demanding.

"Okay," she says simply.

Excitement surges. I jump, yelling with joy, but her sharp glance pulls me back to earth. I calm down.

I joined her for the day, performing temple rituals, meditating at Assi Ghat. A deep peace settles over me. We open our eyes at the same time, our gaze meeting in silence.

Sitting beside her, I ask, "Why do you meditate at different ghats? Why not choose just one?"

She looks at the river, then answers, "You're watching change. I observe the shift."

I frown. "What's the difference?"

She turns, eyes glowing with quiet wisdom.

"Change is movement, from one state to another. Like a leaf falling. A storm passing. But a shift... is internal. It's a transformation of self. Kaashi is sacred. Every ghat holds symbolic energy, each one guiding you from life toward liberation. By meditating at each, I align with that sacred flow. It defines me."

I'm mesmerized. Her words illuminate something vast and divine, something I had only begun to feel.

We continue her routine. Watching her feed street dogs with the food I bring, seeing her simple yet profound acts across Kaashi, my admiration grows.

At Tulsi Ghat, we sit on a stone bench. The sun dips low.

"I'm leaving Kaashi today as well," she says softly.

I'm stunned. "Where are you going?" I ask urgently.

"Himalayas," she replies.

A sudden desire to go with her blooms in me. I hesitate. Then, with effort, ask, "Can I join you? You know I love exploring… and it'll be better with you."

She looks at me, doubtful. "You can come," she says. "But I won't return with you. Is that okay?"

I grin. "Okay."

She smiles, and in that moment, Kaashi's mystic pulse binds us. A new journey begins on the horizon.

Chapter 4

The Route

Sukracharya was in a grand mansion in Paatala Loka, the underworld ruled by demons, discussing and advising Bruthala on his future plans to take control of the universe.

The mansion was terrifying. Massive pillars stood tall, carved with vulgar human figures. These pillars rested on stone elephants, and the walls were covered in horrifying demon sculptures, all painted black. The throne was a gruesome creation, built from human hands and animal legs, covered in black cushions. It was three feet wide and six feet high, surrounded by brass detailing.

As Sukracharya and Bruthala are in deep discussion, news about the brutal war between the demons and *Aghoris* broke out. As his expectation about this war again turns into reality and makes him see another leap of loss, Sukracharya, who was standing and explaining, suddenly collapses into a chair. As the demons around him checked on him for this sudden reaction, Sukracharya was slipping into unconsciousness and simultaneously remembering the real reason why the demons had gone to Mount Kailash.

In Krita Yuga…

The caverns of Patala Loka pulsed with a primal darkness, their seven worlds, Atala, Vitala, Sutala, Rasatala, Talatala, Mahatala, cradled in the universe's shadowed womb. Here, where molten rivers hissed and obsidian spires clawed at the void, Krimi Bandha reigned as king, his power a cosmic inferno that no force dared challenge. His citadel, a fortress of blackened iron wreathed in flames that devoured light, stood as a monument to his dominion. Within its halls, his son, Bruthala, was forged, an unbeatable warrior at fifteen, his eyes twin embers of ambition, his heart a crucible of destiny. The air trembled with his potential, a promise to surpass even his father's legend, tempered by the cruel hand of Sukracharya, the demon sage whose sorcery could unravel stars.

Sukracharya's training was a symphony of pain, each note designed to sculpt Bruthala to become a king who can rule through fear. In chambers where chaos swirled like a living storm, the sage bound Bruthala in chains of starfire, the searing agony of a lover's embrace. "Pain is your crown," Sukracharya rasped, his voice a blade, as Bruthala's screams wove into roars of defiance.

Paatala Loka's laws, conquest, betrayal, dominion, were carved into his soul, each decreed a wound that bled ambition. Krimi Bandha, himself a disciple of Sukracharya's brutal forge, stood watch, his pride a silent thunder. One twilight, in the citadel's throne room, Sukracharya summoned them, his presence a shadow that stilled the flames.

"Bruthala," the sage intoned, his eyes like dying suns, "Patala Loka is but a spark. To claim the cosmos, you must know your foes. Go to Bhumandala, realm of mortals and gods. Learn their laws, their tricks, their hearts. Disguise yourself as one of them, and return with the power to crush them."

Krimi Bandha loomed beside the throne, his horns glinting like crescent moons. He turned to Bruthala, his voice a low rumble, heavy with expectation. "Son, you're going to our enemies' place. Your focus isn't just learning; it's their mindset. Master their traps, and you'll be king of the universe, like me."

"Okay, Father," Bruthala whispered, his voice steady but his chest tight with the weight of his mission.

Krimi Bandha stepped closer, his clawed hand gripping Bruthala's shoulder. His eyes softened, a rare vulnerability breaking through. "Dear Bruthala, take care of yourself," he murmured, his voice a tremor of love amidst the citadel's fire.

The words burned in Bruthala's heart as Sukracharya wove a spell, cloaking his demonic essence in a divine veneer. A family from Patala Loka, bound by the sage's sorcery, was sent to pose as his kin. At fifteen, Bruthala stepped through a rift to Tamraparni, an island in Bhumandala where emerald forests kissed sapphire seas. There, under the tutelage of Brihaspati, guru of the gods, he became Brindhan, a name that danced on mortal lips like a prayer.

In Tamraparni's school, a grove where banyan trees whispered ancient truths, Brindhan was a star. His intellect, sharp as a demon's fang, cut through texts with ease, while his charm, a calculated mask, wove a spell over peers and teachers. He laughed with classmates, shared mangoes under the sun, yet his eyes, ever watchful, cataloged Bhumandala's secrets for Patala's gain. In Brihaspati's classes, Brindhan's answers gleaned with insight. One morning, as sunlight dappled the grove, Brihaspati addressed his students, his voice resonant with wisdom.

"Every nature has its own law," he said, his beard flowing like a river. "We must obey and follow it. It is our responsibility."

Brindhan raised his hand, his voice clear, tinged with a sincerity that masked his true intent. "It is not a condition to be obeyed, Master. We are showing our gratitude toward this nature. Because of it, we formed in our mother's womb, grew in this world, and in the end, the land embraced us. We are grateful for all these gifts."

Brihaspati's eyes shone with approval. "Well said, Brindhan. Your heart sees the divine in the ordinary." The class murmured, and Brindhan bowed, hiding a flicker of triumph, his words, though true, were a tool to deepen his disguise.

Yet, beneath the facade, Brindhan's heart ached for Patala Loka. One moonless night, he sat on Tamraparni's seashore, the waves crashing like his father's voice: *Master their traps, and you'll be king.*

The sea stretched into infinity, a mirror of his ambition. A cry shattered his thoughts, "Save us!", desperate, echoing from the dark waters.

Brindhan jumped up with a fast-beating heart and looked around the empty shore. The calls for help were gone, carried away by the wind. Near the rocks, a lone boat swayed in the surf. He seized it, pushing into the sea, the waves slamming against him like Patala's molten rivers. Thunder roared, the sky a cauldron of darkness, the boat groaning under the storm's wrath. Brindhan rowed, his arms burning, guided by the fading cry. A wave crashed, nearly swallowing him, but his demonic resolve, veiled yet fierce, drove him forward.

Through the tempest, a shadow emerged, a boat, snagged on a reef, a boy his age clinging to its splintered edge. The boy's eyes, wide with terror, met Brindhan's as a wave tore him free. Brindhan lunged, his hand snatching the boy's wrist as the sea claimed him. He hauled him aboard, the boy's body limp, water streaming from his lips. Brindhan pressed his stomach, forcing the water out, until the boy coughed, shuddered, and sank into a restless sleep. Brindhan rowed toward the village, the storm easing as dawn painted the horizon gold.

Hours later, the boy stirred, rubbing his eyes. He saw Brindhan at the boat's edge, steering toward shore. "Who are you?" he asked, voice raw.

"I am Brindhan from Tamraparni," Brindhan said, his tone warm, eyes sharp. "What's your name?"

"I'm Yama. I live here, but I've never seen you."

"I just joined Master Brihaspati's school," Brindhan replied.

Yama nodded

curiosity sparking. "Why were you out there?"

Yama grinned, sheepish. "I wanted to know where this sea ends in the universe. I asked my father, but he forbade it. So, I stole a boat when no one was looking."

Brindhan's laugh rang out, surprising him with its warmth. "Did you find it?"

"Yes," Yama said, eyes twinkling.

"What?"

"My destiny, towards the end."

They laughed, the boat rocking, and Yama hugged Brindhan, a fierce, sudden embrace. "From today, you're my friend," he declared, his voice brimming with joy.

On Tamraparni's shore, their bond took root, a tether in Brindhan's calculated world. He trained under Brihaspati, absorbing cosmic laws and divine strategies, each lesson a weapon for Patala. Outside, he met Yama, sharing food, stories, and a straw mat under the stars. Yama's family welcomed Brindhan, their warmth a strange ache in his chest, while he introduced his Patala-born kin, whispering cautions to maintain their disguise.

One evening, as fireflies danced, Brindhan asked, "Don't you study? Don't you have a teacher?"

Yama gazed at the sky, his voice soft. "I'm my own teacher. Live with the universe, and it guides you."

     Thé Kaashi

Brindhan raised an eyebrow, his tone polished. "Okay." Brindhan didn't buy Yama's words yet ignored that for then and started playfully jumping over the trees and running here and there. Suddenly he fell and cried "***ime'eni***". Yama was startled by two things here: one is the fact that Brindhan fell down and the other is he yelled in a different language he didn't hear of anytime.

By taking care of Brindhan and his wound, Yama was wondering all the time what that word could be. Because anyone in that situation will yell for their mother in their own mother tongue but Brindhan did something very different. Though he wanted to ask Brindhan, he then thought of letting it go and carefully returned carrying Brindhan on his shoulders.

Once they trekked into a forest, plucking mangoes and leaves, tossing them in playful arcs. They ate until their laughter drowned the birdsong. On their path, a lion's corpse lay, its body torn, blood soaking the earth.

Brindhan's heart clenched. "Oh my ***Tjukurrpa..*** It's sad to see that," he murmured. Yama again noticed another new word from Brindhan and now started thinking to ask if he is learning anything new after they complete this trek and head back.

Yama's eyes darkened, thoughtful. "You feel a life's end. I wonder why this creature's end was so cruel."

They pressed on, the forest's weight lingering, and reached a cave, its mouth a vast, shadowed maw. Darkness cloaked its depths, whispers and drips echoing like ghosts. Fear tingled in their bones, but curiosity pulled them inside. Brindhan's voice trembled with awe. "What a wonder in this universe!"

Yama glanced at him, startled by the phrase. Brindhan stepped forward, entranced. "Such a big caaa…" His foot slipped, and he plummeted into a hidden valley, a cry tearing from his throat.

Yama lunged, grabbing for Brindhan's hand, but it slipped away. Morning light pierced the cave, glinting on a stone. Yama spotted a black rope coiled nearby, its surface pulsing with faint energy. He seized it, his fingers tingling, and shouted, "Brindhan!"

Brindhan's voice echoed, raw with fear. "Yama!" Sweat drenched his face as he clung to a jagged ledge, his heart pounding like Patala's drums.

Yama, chest tight with panic, closed his eyes, the cave's darkness and Brindhan's cries a storm in his mind. "Yamaaa!" Brindhan's voice rang out. Yama hurled the rope, guided by the echo, his love for his friend a beacon. It arced true, and Brindhan grasped it, hauling himself up with Yama's desperate pull. They collapsed outside, Brindhan trembling, Yama's arms wrapping him in a fierce, tear-streaked hug.

On a stone outside the cave, they caught their breath, the rope coiled beside Yama. Brindhan's voice was soft, shaken. "Why this rope?"

Yama's eyes glistened. "It saved my friend's life. Wherever I go, it'll be with me, a sign of you."

Brindhan's throat tightened, tears threatening. Yama's gaze grew serious. "I need to ask you something."

"Yes, ask me," Brindhan said, his heart racing.

"You're not from this world," Yama said, his voice steady but searching. "Where are you from?"

Brindhan faltered, the mask he'd worn for years cracking. "No, I'm from here. I belong to this world."

Yama leaned closer, unwavering. "I noticed you speaking some different language and even some of your activities are so strange that I never heard of. Words like, **"ime'eni", "Tjukurrpa"**, That's not what we speak here. Where are you from?"

Brindhan exhaled and decided to reveal himself to his best friend, the truth spilling like blood. "I hid it from you. I'm from Patala Loka. Sukracharya sent me to learn Bhumandala's tricks and rules. My real name is Bruthala. I waited to tell you, but you asked. I'm glad to share now."

Yama fell silent, his heart wrestling. *Is deception dharma? Is this right?* Bruthala saw the storm in his friend's eyes and called, "Yama!"

Yama blinked, his voice heavy with anguish. "I'm sorry. My mind's been tearing itself apart, questioning right and wrong. I don't know my purpose. When I touched this rope, I felt strange energies, unreal, cold. I feel lost, ashamed of my doubts." Tears fell as he collapsed into Bruthala's arms, sobbing.

Bruthala held him, his voice a steady flame. "Don't worry, Yama. Everything leads to good. This is a shift in you, embrace it. Be strong, daring. I'm your friend, always with you." He paused, urgency sharpening his tone. "Please, don't reveal my identity to anyone."

Yama met his gaze, his promise a vow carved in stone. "You saved my life. You're my friend until my end. I'll keep this secret forever. And I swear, whatever help you need for dharma, across all universes, I'll give it, even at the cost of my life."

Bruthala's heart swelled, their bond a rare light in his shadowed soul. Years passed, their friendship became an unbreakable thread. Now in their twenties, they stood transformed, Yama in a lean body wearing a black dhoti and studying the universe's rhythms; Bruthala in a white dhoti, his frame a warrior's, forged by Brihaspati's relentless drills. Yama trained himself, learning from stars and seas, while Brihaspati shaped Bruthala into a warrior unmatched, his mastery of Bhumandala's laws a blade for Patala's conquests.

Days before his departure, Bruthala met Yama by the sea, the waves a soft farewell. "I'm returning to my world soon," he said, his voice steady but heavy.

Yama clasped his shoulder, eyes shining. "Take care, my friend. I'm always with you."

In Patala Loka, Krimi Bandha and Sukracharya greeted Bruthala with a feast that shook the citadel, its flames roaring in triumph. Krimi Bandha bestowed a kingdom upon him, one of the seven worlds, its throne a crucible of power. Bruthala ruled with a savage hand, his reign a tempest of violence. He unleashed chaos on other worlds, wielding the cunning tricks and mental craft he had mastered in Bhumandala to ensnare and torment, each conquest a tribute to his father's pride and Sukracharya's vision. He was not just a beast of fury, he ruled with brute and mind, twisting every lesson from Bhumandala into a weapon of dominion.

In the Dwapara Yuga, Bruthala's name was a curse that shook the cosmos, his power a wildfire that consumed the universe's edges. His thoughts, a labyrinth of unexplainable brilliance, crafted strategies that humbled gods, his cruelty a dark symphony played on the bones of his foes. From Patala Loka's obsidian citadel, he ruled the seven worlds, Atala, Vitala, Sutala, Rasatala, Talatala, Mahatala, with savage glee, his laughter a thunderclap as he drank blood from chalices of shattered stars and tore raw flesh from quivering beasts. His ministers groveled, his warriors trembled, all crushed beneath his iron heel. Sukracharya's warcraft guided his campaigns, each victory a lash against the divine. Yet, within his blackened heart, one light burned: his father, Krimi Bandha, the titan whose love had forged him.

One dusk, as Bruthala surveyed a battlefield littered with divine corpses, a messenger knelt, his voice a broken whisper. "My lord, your father… he has ended his life."

The words struck like a spear, piercing Bruthala's soul. His voice choked, a strangled sob, as tears flooded his eyes, blurring the carnage. Krimi Bandha, his love, his duty, his muse, the very pulse of his existence, was gone. A chasm yawned within him, swallowing purpose, leaving only despair. He staggered to his father's mansion, Patala's flames dimming in his grief. Amidst ancient scrolls and relics, he unearthed the truth: Krimi Bandha, burdened by a cosmic prophecy, had chosen death to shield Patala from a looming cataclysm. The revelation shattered Bruthala, his heart splintering as he grasped why his invincible father had embraced such a horrific end.

Rage erupted, a volcanic surge. He stormed Sukracharya's chamber, his roar cracking the walls. "You knew his fate!" he bellowed, tears streaming. "Why didn't you save him? Bring him back, Master! Your sorcery bends the stars, bring him back!"

Sukracharya's eyes, like fading suns, held his gaze. "Some paths are beyond my power, Bruthala. Even I cannot defy death's law."

"Liar!" Bruthala screamed, hurling a throne into the void. "You've failed him, and you betray me!" His grief twisted into a sharper cruelty, his soul a furnace of anguish. He turned away, vowing to reshape the cosmos to his will.

Weeks bled into months, Bruthala's depression a bottomless void. Krimi Bandha's absence haunted him, a specter in every shadow. Madness gripped him, his obsession with his father a fire that scorched reason. He challenged warriors across the universe, their blood soaking his hands, each killing a futile bid to prove the impossible possible.

In his citadel, he shouted looking at the sky for gods, "You call yourselves eternal?" he spat, his voice venomous. "You're nothing! Weak, spineless, cowering before my blade! The universe kneels to me, not your pathetic light!" He crushed a deity's essence, its scream a hymn to his wrath, the divine council trembling as he cursed all existence. "Every star, every soul, every breath, you're all worms beneath my feet!"

Then, a rumor pierced his despair: Yama, his childhood friend from Tamraparni, now reigned over life and death, a cosmic judge in his own dynasty. Hope, raw and jagged, flared in Bruthala's chest. He journeyed to Yama's realm, a fortress where the air pulsed with boiled blood and dread. Black pillars, draped in molten gold, towered, carved with granite figures of divine beings, swastikas, and weapons that glowed with spiritual might. Stone statues, human-shaped, clutched eternal flames, their eyes glinting with ghostly life. The entrance, a door ninety-nine feet high and twenty-seven feet wide, bore square panels and bells that tolled mournfully. Yama's soldiers, armored in death's shimmer, stood sentinel. Inside, a vast hall lay empty, minister chairs lining its edges, leading to Yama's throne, a platinum buffalo, radiant with authority.

Yama, alerted to Bruthala's arrival, descended in regal splendor, his presence a divine storm. Their eyes locked, tears welling, memories of togetherness flooding back. They embraced, a fierce hug that bridged eons, their hearts pounding with shared history. Bruthala, once clad in animal hides, wore a black dhoti, his long beard framing a grief-ravaged face, his titanium crown a cold weight. Yama, adorned in gold bracelets and chains, his dhoti gleaming, sported a powerful mustache, his diamond-studded crown a beacon of dominion.

The feast was a nostalgic tapestry, vegetarian dishes of rice, lentils, and mangoes, a mirror of their Tamraparni days. Yama, speechless with joy, gazed at Bruthala, his friend reborn yet shadowed by sorrow. They laughed, recalling boyhood adventures, but Bruthala's heart bled, his father's loss a wound that festered.

In the hall, Bruthala's gaze fell on a black rope hanging on the wall, its fibers pulsing faintly. "This rope saved me," he murmured, his voice thick with memory.

Yama's eyes glistened. "I've named it Yamapaasa. You recall, I said it surged with energy when I held it. This rope shaped my path, lessons, turns, all because of you. I'm forever grateful."

Bruthala smiled, pride warming him, but his voice fell, heavy with desperation. "Yama, I need your help now."

Yama leaned forward, his vow unshaken. "Ask, Bruthala. Anything for you. I swore for dharma, and I'm always with you."

Bruthala's throat tightened, tears brimming. "You know my father died recently. I'm nothing without him, Yama. He was my supreme, my inspiration, my everything. Can you bring him back?"

Yama's face darkened, torn by duty. "Bruthala, my friend, what you ask defies dharma. I'm helpless. I cannot break that law, not even for you."

Bruthala's hope crumbled, he pleaded. "Please, Yama, I beg you!"

Desperation turned to rage, his cruelty unleashed. "You gods, you divine fools, you think you're above me?" he roared, pacing the hall. "I've crushed your kind, bled your heavens dry! The universe is mine to command, and you, Yama, you're no better, clinging to your petty dharma while I burn!" His voice shook the pillars, bells clanging wildly. "Every existence, gods, mortals, stars, they're nothing! I'll tear it all down if you deny me!"

Yama listened, his patience a taut thread, his eyes steady but smoldering. Bruthala's tirade raged on, cursing creation itself. "You're all dust! I'll grind every soul, every divine spark, under my heel!"

Finally, Yama's restraint snapped, his voice a thunderclap that silenced the hall. "Enough, Bruthala! You're a bloody demon, spitting on our bond!" He rose, his buffalo throne gleaming, his aggression a divine inferno. "My friendship was a gift, yet you curse me? I'm the supreme arbiter, master of all beings! I could end you here, you slave of petty worlds!"

Bruthala's eyes blazed, his voice venomous. "You dare wield your title against me? In days, I'll seize the universe, shatter your dharmas, and rule with my laws! This is my challenge!"

He stormed from the hall, the bells screaming in his wake, his heart a cauldron of betrayal. He plotted to raze Yama's dynasty, armies, sorcery, traps, but each scheme crumbled, Yama's power an unbreakable wall.

In Patala, Sukracharya, informed of the clash, saw an opportunity. Bruthala's rage was a weapon to wield. He waited, bidding time until Bruthala returned, his heart a storm of betrayal. In the citadel's hall, Bruthala raged, his voice shaking the flames. "How dare he reject my wish! My father was like his father, too, wasn't he? He knows the pain, yet denies me! I feel his father is like mine!" He froze, realization dawning, and turned to Sukracharya, eyes wild. "Oh, his father never ends, the universe, the sun itself! That's why he's blind to bonds! I'll fight every divine being, every creator, every destroyer! I'll crush Yama, take his charge, and bring my father back! My word will be reality!"

Sukracharya's lips curled, his voice smooth. "We can take the universe without war, Bruthala."

Bruthala, stunned, leaned closer. "How?"

Sukracharya's eyes gleamed. "An element exists on Bhuloka. If we claim it, we can bend reality, do anything." Bruthala's heart surged, a new fire kindling.

Decades passed, and at the beginning of Kaliyuga, Bruthala had frustratedly confronted Sukracharya.

"We have searched every corner of the universe," Bruthala growled. "We have examined every corner in *Bhuloka* (earth). Is this element even real? Or have you been deceiving us?"

Angered by Bruthala's doubts, Sukracharya grabbed a knife and hurled it at him. Bruthala dodged just in time.

"Look into my eyes. These are the witnesses," Sukracharya roared. "The element is on *Bhuloka*. I know it, but it's against Lord Shiva's will and will not be that easy. Understand!"

Sukracharya had performed countless rituals since Kruta Yuga, searching for this element. He had tried everything, worship, penance, predictions, sacrifices, spying, trickery, and even traps. He and his demons had visited earth millions of times but never found it. Billions of demons had died in the search and even as ritual sacrifices. No matter what he did and how many tricks he used, he failed, era after era.

Because of this row of failures from centuries, consumed by frustration and rage, he stormed towards the sacred chamber of Lord Shiva, the supreme deity of Paatala Loka. He kept looking at Lord Shiva's idol, standing tall at 25 feet, carved as part of the cave. He began a powerful ritual, chanting mantras, pouring drums of milk and water over Shiva's idol, and showering it with fresh white and red jimine flowers, Lord Shiva's favourites in Paatala Loka. He lit a sacred lamp, burned incense, and offered Mirin, a special sweet that Lord Shiva loved.

But there was no response. Sukracharya could not feel anything from Lord Shiva, not even a sign of acknowledgement.

Growing desperate, Sukracharya grabbed his sword and stood before Shiva's idol. His voice trembled with devotion and fury as he praised God with every word he knew. His eyes burned red, filled with both anger and sorrow. Nothing worked. Shiva remained silent.

Shukracharaya said, "Hey Lord Shiva, you've been the only one we have been praying to and worshipping since this world existed. No one can come close to matching our devotion and belief in you. Still, you remained unmoved."

At last, Sukracharya raised his sword, ready to sacrifice his own life.

The moment the blade touched his neck, Lord Shiva appeared before him.

His appearance was marvelous. The idol of Lord Shiva slowly transformed into a living form. As the stone eyes opened, they became real, deep, peaceful, and filled with divine artistry. The Rudraksha beads on his hands turned into real flesh. The blue mark on his neck pulsed with life, glowing softly. The tiger skin covering his body shifted, its fur moving with the wind. A wild snake, black with glowing spots, coiled around his neck, hissing as it came to life. Once carved in stone, the thick hair on his legs became real. His trident, the mighty Trishul, shimmered and solidified into its true form, radiating divine energy.

Shiva's face was beyond words, calm, powerful, yet filled with kindness. Sukracharya stood as a rock, watching this amazing wonder unfold in front of his eyes. Once Shiva appeared in human form, Sukracharya automatically started praying and praising him with songs and writings from his own scriptures he had penned ages ago. He forgot himself and carried on for hours like that.

Lord Shiva looked at Sukracharya and smiled, "What is your wish?" Shiva asked, bringing Sukracharya from his trance.

"Hey Mahadev, you know what I am up to and what stops me from getting it. Please shower your love on me by letting me know the whereabouts of the element I am searching for on this Bhulok," he lowered his tone and requested humbly.

Meanwhile, as we waited for the train to Gorakhpur, I turned to her and asked, "How long does it take to reach the Himalayas from here?"

She smiled and replied, "We'll travel by train, bus, rickshaw, and then trek on foot." It felt as if it would be a very long and tiring journey, which also reflected on my facial expression. She noticed and asked, "So, how much time are you willing to spend with me?"

Her words struck me like a sudden gust, stirring a quiet unease that bloomed into hesitation. I faltered, my response half-formed, when Elena appeared on the platform, her silhouette framed against the fading light. Her gaze found mine, steady and searching, and she approached with a grace that belied the weight she carried. "Ele," I ventured, my voice tentative, "how did you find your way here?"

She paused, her eyes clouding with memory. "That day you inquired about Kaashi, I was adrift, uncertain. My father passed away ten days ago."

A jolt of sorrow caught me. "My God," I murmured, the words barely escaping.

She continued, her voice soft yet resolute. "A distant kin from India sent word, a letter claiming we hold title to assets unknown to us. My father, consumed by his labors, never knew. And then I thought of you, how you seek not the unknown, but the truths we're unaware of possessing."

She turned to depart, then hesitated, glancing back. "I owe you an apology, dear friend. My husband laid bare the secrets I kept, and I'm ashamed of my actions, my choices."

George, her husband, approached then, his smile a fleeting warmth. He clapped my shoulder lightly before retreating into the crowd. Kaashi, I thought, wove its strange enchantment, impossible tides shifting in unforeseen ways. An aghori stood nearby, his unblinking stare piercing through the clamor as the train's iron wail announced its arrival. Without another word, we boarded, the platform's chaos fading behind us.

As the journey began, the train easing from the station, we settled into our seats. Elena chose the window, her presence luminous even in the dim carriage. She was resplendent today, draped in a sapphire saree that cascaded with quiet elegance, her dupatta resting delicately over one shoulder. Her fair complexion glowed, a small tilak on her forehead catching the light like a whispered prayer. Her ears, soft as petals, shimmered faintly as she turned to me. Her eyes, tranquil yet profound, held a warmth that stirred my soul, and her smile, radiant, unguarded, sent my heart skittering.

"What do you do?" she asked, her voice a gentle melody, laced with curiosity.

"I serve with the Security Agency," I replied, steadying my tone.

She tilted her head, her gaze sharpening. "Who are they? What happened?"

Back in the spring of 1990, the world seemed to hold its breath for Elena and me, our love a fragile bloom amid the final days of our university studies. Her eyes, alight with admiration, often sought mine with an intensity that made my heart stutter. One crisp afternoon, as we lingered beneath the ancient oaks lining the campus quad, she turned to me, her voice soft yet probing. "What path will you choose, now that our studies are nearly done?"

I gazed beyond the horizon, where the world stretched into mysteries yet uncovered. "I want to chase something uncharted," I said, my words tentative, as if testing the weight of a dream. "Something unknown, a purpose I can't yet name but feel burning within me."

Elena's laughter was a melody, bright and unburdened. In a swift motion, she straddled my lap, her arms encircling me in a fierce embrace. "Whatever you seek, I'll stand by you until my last breath," she whispered, her breath warm against my ear. "But promise me you'll find steady work, something to build a life on, so we can marry."

I nodded, my heart swelling with her faith in me. "Okay," I murmured, and our lips met in a kiss that sealed a vow, fragile as it was fervent.

Days later, the weight of the world shifted. George, a steadfast friend and Elena's confidant, arrived at my dormitory with a letter clutched in his hand. Its edges were worn, the handwriting unmistakably my mother's. I tore it open, my pulse quickening.

Dear Son,

I pray you're well. Here, the tides have turned against us. The businesses have collapsed under the weight of dwindling finances. Peter, your stepfather, has squandered what little we had, amassing debts that now choke us, a hundred thousand dollars, with my name bound as guarantor. I rue the day I chose him after your father's passing. Enclosed are a few dollars to sustain you. Finish your degree, but please, return home swiftly. I need you now.

Love you always,

Mother

The words carved a hollow in my chest. Her despair, inked in every trembling stroke, seeped into me. For days, I drifted in silence, my thoughts a tempest Elena could not penetrate. She pressed me with questions, her concern a quiet ache, but I offered no answers. As my final semester drew to a close, I resolved to leave, alone, without a word to her, believing distance would spare her the burden of my fractured future.

On the eve of my departure, George found me packing in the dim light of my room. His voice was steady, but his eyes betrayed worry. "What about Elena?" he asked.

I paused, my back to him, the weight of her love pressing against my resolve. "If she marries me, she'll suffer a lifetime tethered to my failures," I said, my voice low. "If she marries another, her pain will fade as I become a distant memory."

Time moved forward, as it always does, relentless and unyielding. I learned later that Elena had married George, a man whose kindness rivaled the goodness I'd always admired in him. My heart, though bruised, found solace in their union, a quiet joy that she'd found a worthy companion.

The revelation that Elena had married George, my truest friend whose soul shone with uncommon kindness, had once brought me a quiet joy, a balm for the ache of letting her go. I had believed her happiness secured, her life unburdened by the shadows of my past.

Yet, as the years unfolded, that certainty unraveled. Weeks ago, in a café brimming with the clamor of life, Elena's gaze had pierced through me, her words sharp with accusation. She had scolded me, her voice trembling with the pain of my unexplained departure, a wound I now knew George had laid bare with his honest heart.

"What stirs such sorrow in you, wanderer?" she asked, her voice a gentle current, carrying the wisdom of Kaashi's eternal embrace. Her eyes, deep as the cosmos, fixed on mine.

My vision blurred with unshed tears, and I began to speak, my words a confession woven with the threads of my journey. "She was my love, once," I said, my voice barely rising above the marketplace's din. "I left her to shield her from a life entangled in my family's ruin, debts and despair that would have chained her dreams. I thought her pain would fade, that I'd become a forgotten echo. But seeing her now, her regret mirroring my own, I wonder if I only sowed a deeper sorrow." I paused, my gaze drifting to the spires of Kaashi's temples, their ancient stones whispering of redemption. "Yet this city, this sacred Kaashi, has taught me gratitude for the paths I've walked, however broken. Its ghats and prayers have shown me that every choice, even those steeped in sacrifice, carves the soul toward purpose. I am grateful for this clarity, for the chance to see her again, to know that our stories, though parted, still ripple through time."

The aghori nodded, her weathered face etched with understanding, as my tears fell like offerings to the eternal city that had both broken and remade me.

pausing before adding, "What inspired you to choose this path?"

"Choose what?" she asked, her brow furrowing in confusion.

"Aghori," I clarified softly, unsure how she'd take it.

She gazed out the window, her expression growing distant as her thoughts seemed to drift back in time, lost in the past.

"At the age of two, I lost both my parents in a tragic accident. From that moment on, my grandfather, my father's father, became everything to me. He was a Hindu priest by profession; he served at the temple and became my sole guardian. He cared for me, being my father, mother, teacher, and friend whenever needed. Because of his devotion to his work, I loved worshipping the gods. I would often ask him endless questions about the divine, eager to hear the stories he would share."

Every night, without fail, he would sit with me and tell the story of gods and goddesses. One evening, unable to contain my curiosity, I asked him, "Grandpa... During massive wars, gods carry weapons, but why do they carry musical instruments?"

Grandpa smiled and replied, "Weapons may control your behaviour, but instruments can awaken your soul."

At ten, I remember one day playing hide-and-seek with my friends. I hid far away in an abandoned old building far from the village. The place was dark and surrounded by dense forest, so I lost my way. After a while, I began to cry loudly, my sobs echoing in the emptiness. I sat down, overwhelmed by fear and confusion, not knowing what to do. Time seemed to stretch endlessly. Eventually, exhaustion took over, and I fell asleep right there.

When I woke up, the fear still gripped me, and tears filled my eyes. But then, I noticed something, something unusual. I reached out and picked it up. It was old, delicate, and felt oddly significant. Just as I held it, I heard voices calling my name. The villagers, including my grandpa, arrived, and I could see the deep worry on his face. He had been searching for me since morning.

I was overjoyed to see them, and my grandpa's face lit up with relief as he saw me. The villagers, too, breathed a collective sigh of relief. As I handed my grandpa the strange, antique object, his eyes widened in astonishment. Tears welled up in his eyes as he gazed at it, and he began thanking God aloud, his voice filled with gratitude. The object I had found was no ordinary trinket; it was the lost earring of Goddess Parvati from the temple.

It had been missing for several years. The villagers, along with my grandpa, were deeply saddened by its disappearance. Goddess Parvati herself had given the earring during the Kritha Yuga as a token of recognition for the establishment of her idol in the village temple. The village, known as Taatankam, is located near the Himalayas. Each year, the villagers celebrated in honour of the goddess, offering their prayers and seeking her blessings.

However, during Kali Yuga, disaster struck. One day, a thief stole one of the goddess's earrings. As he tried to steal the second earring, the villagers arrived at the temple in time to notice. In his haste to escape, the thief dropped the earring, and it fell into the depths of the land. The loss devastated the village, and they decided not to celebrate the festival again until the missing earring was found. The villagers placed the remaining earring aside, keeping it safe, and waited in sorrow.

Years later, I wandered off and stumbled upon the earring. The discovery of this sacred object marked the end of the village's sorrow. With it, the long-awaited celebrations could finally begin again. As the villagers, including my grandpa, marvelled at the earring, we all realised that the goddess had, in her own way, brought us back together, restoring both the festival and the joy that had been missing for so long.

Five years later, my grandpa sat in the temple, reading through his palmistry texts in front of Lord Shiva. As he read, he came across something new that caught his attention. I walked in, calling out, "Grandpa..."

"Come here, dear. What do you need?" he asked, looking up with a smile.

"My teacher asked what I want to be when I grow up. What is your wish for me, Grandpa?" I asked, curious.

He thought momentarily before answering, "I wish for you to be a child of God, a child of Lord Shiva."

While she shared her story, we reached the final stage of our route, the mountain. She suddenly stopped speaking, and I could see tears in her eyes. She was avoiding me, trying to hide her feelings. So, to clear the air and change the mood, I stopped and breathed while we were hiking the mountain. I took out a water bottle and sipped water.

"So, you chose this profession for your grandpa?" I asked loudly, with a bit of a laugh, keeping my bottle back in the bag.

She nodded with a serious expression but didn't speak.

We're hiking to a place she showed on a map when we were on the bus. It is almost at the top of a mountain that stands at 8000 feet, and we need to do rope climbing to reach it. We're currently at 7000 feet already, but it's getting tougher as we climb higher, and the path ahead is also becoming unclear.

After several hours, we finally reached our destination. At the top, we found a huge temple, almost like a mansion. The architecture was amazing, unlike anything I had ever seen. Every sculpture on the walls and pillars was incredible, especially the animal figures. Some animals looked completely different from any I'd seen before, with features that seemed impossible, as if they belonged to another time. The carvings showed people from ancient times, saints, sages, women, children, all detailed in almost lifelike ways.

Manuscripts were written on the walls, and the morning sunlight made everything look even more beautiful. Despite its remote location high in the mountains, the temple was clean and well-kept.

I was mesmerised by everything I saw, stepping forward in awe. She had fallen a few metres behind me, looking around carefully. Though it was not of her kind, as I never saw her before doing it, I neglected it as my heart and mind were pushing me more towards exploring this ancient wonder. I could feel some sort of connection to this monument, and I felt like I was getting pulled by it rather than going in on my own will.

As I was lost in the beauty of the temple's external architecture and started heading inside, I noticed another person in the temple. He was examining something on one of the pillars. Suddenly, he raised his voice.

"There's no more time for us, Veda. How long will you take to bring him here?" he asked.

He was speaking to the *Aghori*, and I watched in shock as she removed her dupatta and saree, revealing that she was dressed in jeans and a shirt. She looked nothing like the spiritual figure I had been with. I couldn't believe my eyes.

"Sorry, sir," she replied calmly, "he took longer than I expected." She then pulled a gun from her pocket and aimed it at me. I understood that I was trapped. The man left the temple while this girl made me kneel.

As they started discussing something, I tried to recreate the power I experienced underwater in Kaashi, hoping to use it to escape from them. Though I couldn't do it instantly, I started feeling something within me, and some flashes from my underwater dip experience started to strike me faintly, from the 3 dips. I started remembering more than what I explained to my buddy, Carlos and this aghori, sorry fake aghori - veda.

Chapter 5

The Power

I was on my knees, hands trembling, as Veda held a gun to my head at point-blank range. Right before me was Anand with a piercing gaze. He was a short man in a khaki safari suit,with a clean moustache and a tilak on his forehead.

"Who are you guys? Why have you trapped me?" I pleaded. "I'm not even a billionaire! I'm just a loyal debtor to the bank. Please, let me go. I'm a responsible citizen of my country!"

"Shut up!!" Veda snapped and pushed the gun in my mouth.

"Okay!, okay!," I raised my hands to surrender and told them, "At least you could do is, let me call my friend and take out an insurance policy on my name and then you can do whatever you guys want"

Anand Kanipakam let out a cold laugh before his expression quickly shifted to anger. "Where is it?" he demanded.

I blinked in confusion. "The company? It's in Mexico. Its policies offer great benefits. Do you want me to explain?"

"You idiot!" he thundered. "I'm asking about Kaashidhara!"

I frowned. "Kaashidhara? Is that a place or a thing?"

"He's acting smart, Veda!!. Treat him our way to get the truth out," Anand growled.

Veda immediately replied, "I don't think he knows about it, Anand. I never heard him speak about it. Let me find out if he remembers anything."

"Do whatever it takes, I need progress!! Veda, I am leaving to observe the temple" Anand spoke firmly and left.

Veda pulled out a map and spread it before me. I glanced at it and said, "Wait... you showed me this map on the bus, right? I asked you to take me there! So, are you asking me about the location of a place where I asked you to take me? Ah, it's so funny. How would you think I know where it is?"

I sighed in frustration and continued, "Listen, I'm from Mexico. I didn't know where India or Kaashi was, yet I found my way here. And now you're talking about some Kaashidhara in the Himalayas? I don't even know that such a place exists! Why are you doing this to me?"

Veda was about to tell me something, and I stopped her this time and continued, "I demand answers from both of you!" I yelled aggressively. "Who are you? And what's the real story behind all of this?"

Veda took a deep breath and explained the rest of the story, "listen to me carefully and shut your mouth till I complete"

I have always been fascinated with collecting ancient relics of gods and goddesses. It all started after I discovered the lost earrings of Goddess Parvati. From then on, I was drawn to antiques wherever I could find them. At first, it was just a hobby, but over time, it turned into a passion.

One day, I asked my grandfather about his greatest wish for my future. He gave me his answer, but the very next day, he made a startling discovery. While studying ancient palmistry scripts written by the great sage Tulsidas, he found a reference to a mysterious element of Lord Shiva, one that still exists on earth. Surprised by this revelation, he kept the information to himself.

Not long after, three scientists from the Indian Mythological Antiques Department visited my grandfather, who was also looking for the very same element. They even offered a handsome amount as a reward if he could help them find and obtain it. My grandfather, an ardent devotee of Lord Shiva, strongly believes that divine things should only be with the gods but not in the hands of others. He sent them back without sharing any information about the element that he was aware of.

My grandfather decided to protect the secrecy of that element for the rest of his life, and he succeeded in doing so. They tried convincing him, while I was returning from school I stopped by the temple and as my grandfather was stubborn and he requested them to not trouble him and they returned in disappointment. After watching all of this, I curiously asked my grandfather, "who are they?"

He explained who they were and what they did. That day, I learned that there is a dedicated department of government that works to find our lost ancient glory by discovering clues and things from ages past. That response intrigued me. I thought that would be one of my interests: finding and knowing our history.

As I was thinking all these things, my grandfather called me near and whispered in my ear that the element of Lord Shiva they were searching for does exist on this earth. I was stunned. Before I could ask more, he took my hands and made me promise to find this element and return it to Lord Shiva. I swore to fulfil his wish. The moment I made that promise, he smiled wholeheartedly. I could sense a lot of relief and belief on his face. But he didn't move from there; his body stiffened, and he collapsed before me. A sudden heart failure took his life right then and there.

Grief-stricken and not knowing what to do, I clutched the ancient palmistry scripts and ran after the scientists' car, desperate to catch up. I ran so fast that I coughed, shouted, and waved at them to stop. Finally, one of the scientists noticed me, stopped, and stepped out of the car.

As they started enquiring about me, asking all sorts of questions, I was trying to catch my breath. It was becoming difficult for me to talk immediately as my lungs burned from the chase. After a few seconds, I barely managed to tell them, "the element you were looking for does exist on earth." I bargained for the clue, my grandfather found to get included in their team.

I looked at Veda with a very puzzled expression; it instantly conveyed my feelings about her trading something her grandfather valued more than his life right after she lost him.

Veda continued and looked as if she understood what I was thinking about her, "Yes, I know what you are thinking about me. I feel very ashamed now, but then, I didn't know what I was doing as I was a child and naive. They promised that they'd let me join their team once I completed my education, but as I insisted on being with them, they agreed to allow me to work with them unofficially."

I replied, "You betrayed your grandfather. Don't you feel any regret?"

Anand and Veda exchanged glances before continuing the story.

After that day, I continued my studies in school, but my real focus was elsewhere. Indian Mythological Anitques Department (IMAD) assigned a team to assist me and I began this journey by starting the first ever investigation by analysing the scriptures my grandfather studied. One of them was Aranyaka Scripture, written by Tulsidas.

My grandfather, being a Vedic scholar, had a deep understanding of these scriptures. He even taught me how to read them a few years before his passing. But no matter how much I tried, I couldn't understand how he had deciphered the location of Lord Shiva's element.

I spent days, nights, weeks, months, years, even obsessing over the palm-leaf manuscripts. Then, after two long years, I discovered something incredible. Hidden within the text, some letters formed the shape of a Shiva idol. They were all reversed and underlined.

I copied these letters onto a whiteboard, arranging them carefully. "Dha", "Shi" , "Ra", "Kaa"

That's when it hit me, the text revealed a name: Kaashidhara. I was so overjoyed that I progressed, and my efforts for this long time fetched something positive. But it didn't last long as I searched for Kaashidhara and found nothing about it, be it online, in the department, or in scriptures.

We were in a dilemma of what Kaashidhara could be, whether it is a place, a relic, or something beyond our imagination and expectation, a divine creation. No one in the department could find any historical or scriptural evidence of its existence. Eventually, we concluded that it was nothing more than a theory. The Aranyaka scripture was, after all, a translated Vedic text, perhaps Kaashidhara was just another poetic metaphor lost in time. Disappointed, we moved on.

Years later, I completed my postgraduate studies in Vedic Literature and Archaeological Sciences. Before officially joining IMAD, I embarked on a journey of self-discovery to the Himalayas.

While I was in Kathmandu, few locals guided me to a secluded temple which was built on a grand scale like a castle. They cautioned me that reaching the castle was a steep climb, it was not for the faint hearted and every few got to climb the castle up and never returned.

Back then, I looked completely different. I wore torn jeans, a collarless T-shirt, a nose piercing, and stylish earrings. My skin was pale, and my long, loose hair flowed in the mountain winds. I had no idea that this journey would change everything.

Determined, I set off alone, though learning about its history was a bit scary. The journey took 14 grueling hours. Along the way, I took breaks, ate, read my book, and even napped. Finally, I reached the temple.

The sight inside left me speechless. The architecture was breathtaking, the inscriptions engraved on the walls mesmerising. I took several snapshots for reference.

Then, standing before a 20-foot idol of a sleeping man, I experienced something surreal.

A small piece of cloth floated towards me, carried by the wind. I caught it, unrolled it, and to my astonishment, it was a map: a route leading to Kaashidhara.

I was stunned. The name Kaashidhara – I had seen it before.

Instantly, I remembered the Aranyaka scripture. I took it out, compared the markings, and everything aligned.

This new discovery made me want to return to the department immediately and in two weeks I was back.

For the first time, we had a real lead. We had proof that Kaashidhara was real.

In our department, we were a pretty small team : me, Anand, Ramesh, Gurumurthy and Satish. Together we embarked on a mission to uncover the truth behind kaashidhara.

The map we had discovered was written in Sanskrit. Its design was a long, winding S-shape, with seven key points marked using ancient mantra symbols: Kaashi, Saga, Dhruthi Parvat, Kaashidhara, Parvathi Stal, Gauri Kund, and Kaashi.

At first glance, it made no sense. The element was supposed to be at Kaashidhara, yet the map seemed to trace a journey from Kaashi to Kaashi. "What did this mean? Was Kaashidhara a hidden place within Kaashi, or was there a deeper, symbolic meaning we had yet to decode?"

We explored every possible interpretation for three long years, tested countless theories, and followed every lead. But nothing worked. No breakthrough, no answers, just a frustrating loop that always brought us back to the beginning.

We were right where we had started.

Determined to uncover the truth, I decided to go to Kaashi as an *Aghori* and search for answers myself. Every day and every passing minute, I chased after any lead, hoping to find even the smallest clue about Kaashidhara.

For the past year, I have lived in Kaashi, questioning sages, saints, and even *Aghoris*, but no one has ever heard of Kaashidhara. It was as if it never existed.

"Then, one day, I saw you on a boat. At first, I didn't pay much attention to you, but then I found your wallet and mobile in the boat. While returning them to you, it struck me that I've seen you somewhere when standing up close."

"Where did you see me? Possibly on the streets themselves... but the main important question is, Why are you abusing me now? let me out of here, I don't want to be trapped!!" I yelled aggressively at veda.

She looked at me with a mix of frustration and desperation. "Because I had lost all hope. It's been twelve years, twelve long years of searching for something that might not even exist. And then, one day, I overheard you on the phone, telling your friend about the power you experienced in the Ganges River."

"So what?" I shot back.

"In this map, we noticed three coded symbols mark the path to Kaashidhara," she answered.

"What do they mean?" I asked, my curiosity now piqued.

"At first, we didn't pay much attention to these codes," Veda said. "But in your first dip, you saw the power in your hand."

She pointed to one corner of the map. "Here, it says: Power in the hand under the water, he who possesses it can create or destroy anything in the universe."

A memory flashed through my mind. That day, when the stone came rushing towards me, I destroyed it and then created the exact same stone again. It was completely under my control, but I had hidden this truth from her.

"In the second dip, you saw all the planets in the river," she continued, tracing her finger to another corner of the map. "Everything is governed by the *Pancha Mahabhutas*, the five great elements. But when you tried to destroy them, you lost your power."

She wasn't entirely right. I had concealed something else.

I didn't just see the planets – I absorbed their energy. Every planet's power merged into me, making my strength limitless.

"And in the third dip, you saw Goddess Kalika," she said, pointing to the final corner of the map. "When you saw her, you were terrified and rushed out of the river."

But that wasn't the whole truth either.

I closed my eyes, reliving that moment.

The Goddess Kalika stood before me, her presence overwhelming. I had never felt such immense power before.

"You have come here for a purpose," she told me. "This infinite power will remain with you... until you reach your destination. You will be reloaded with it whenever needed."

"What is my destination?" I asked eagerly.

"Kaashidhara," she replied. And just like that, she vanished.

But it never worked no matter how often I tried to use my power in Kaashi. Every day, I tested it, again and again, only to be exhausted and disappointed.

Then, the moment Veda mentioned the Himalayas, something inside me stirred. Maybe... just maybe, my power would work there. That thought alone made me eager to go.

The day before, I glanced at the map in Veda's hands on the bus and saw the name Kaashidhara marked. In Kaashi, I asked people to write the name in Hindi so I could inquire about it. Some words seemed to match, but I needed to dig deeper.

Without hesitation, I turned to Veda and said, "Take me there."

And now, here I am - trapped.

I needed to know if my power was still working. Slowly, I shifted my hands behind my back, careful not to draw anyone's attention. I clenched my fists, then opened them again.

A faint pulse of energy coursed through my palms. I focused and felt it intensify.

Yes.

It's working.

A slow smile crept across my face. Though I immediately wanted to get rid of them using power and escape from that place, one thing was stopping me. 'The Element'

I needed to know how something that is so mythological is related to lord shiva and how does it fit with someone born in mexico with no roots connected to indian mythological history.

Chapter 6

The Element

The remaining three officers arrived at the field. They gave their reports, and Ramesh spoke first.

"We didn't find any place or person named Kaashidhara," he said.

Gurumurthy added, "We asked the locals, but no one knew anything."

Satish sighed. "That means he's the only one who can tell us what it is and where to find it."

Everyone except Anand was in uniform, black jeans and light brown shirts. They all looked strong and fit, like trained officers. But Anand was different. He was short, overweight, and didn't look like he belonged on a field mission. He seemed more like a funny guy than a serious officer.

As they continued discussing the element, I decided to clarify about everything that is going on.

"I have a question," I said.

Gurumurthy turned to me. "What is it?"

"Can you tell me what exactly this element you're looking for?"

Ramesh suddenly grabbed my collar and pointed a gun at me. His voice was full of anger.

"Are you trying to fool us? If you don't tell us where Kaashidhara is, we'll kill you!" he shouted.

I raised my hands slightly. "Relax, relax," I said with a small smile. "You guys are expecting much from me. I asked her to bring me here, but I don't know Kaashi, I don't know India. Honestly, until I landed here, I didn't know this place existed. I didn't like history in my childhood."

Satish got frustrated with my words and shoved his gun into my mouth.

Just then, I tilted my head slightly, and my eyes were in shock.

Demons.

They were clinging on to the ceiling of the mansion-temple, watching us silently and stalking us. A chill ran down through me. The moment they realised I had seen them, they let out a terrifying scream and attacked us.

Everything turned into chaos.

One of them leaped directly at me. Instinctively, I unleashed my powers and obliterated the demon in an instant.

Veda and her team were in shock, both at the demons and at my power.

Veda, especially, was stunned. How did my powers activate again? She couldn't believe what she was seeing.

Was this real? Was it just a fantasy? Or was I something beyond human, something supernatural?

But before she could think any further, more demons appeared.

There was no time to process it.

She grabbed her weapon and started attacking.

Anand screamed in fear. Ramesh and Satish started shooting at the demons, their guns firing rapidly. But for every demon they shot down, another three spawned disgustingly out of its stomach, multiplying instantly.

Within seconds, the entire place was filled with demons and their foul stench. They surrounded me. I clenched my fists, feeling a surge of energy rushing through my body. It's time to fight!!.

When two demons charged at me simultaneously, I released my power through my palms, pushing it forcefully with all my force. I continued rotating, unleashing my energy without stopping. Suddenly, the demons began regenerating from my power, I tried closing my hands and opening them again. The power shuts off, but when I repeat the action, the power surges back on, and I can destroy them repeatedly. Doing this took a tool on my hands as it aches from the strain I put on them and I can no longer generate power for longer periods of time. After a few seconds, the demons were recreated again from the same source. Exhausted, I turned my energy down and turned them back again, but this time I realized something, I needed to give myself breaks before recreating them. I must endure the pain, no matter how intense,cruel because the lives of those around me are at risk. I need to control myself and my power to handle this situation.

Anand was watching from the corner, too scared to fight, completely frozen by the demons. I couldn't stop laughing, thinking back how he acted all mighty when we first met, and now looking at him, shaking in fear, trembling. I felt bad for him but before I knew it, four demons surrounded me. Ramesh and Gurumurthy had already given up, trapped and helpless, and the demons were about to kill them.

Two demons spotted Anand, grabbed him and dragged him into the field. He screamed for help, his voice filled with panic, "Please save me!!!"

Satish was stuck between three demons, barely able to protect himself. Veda ran out of bullets and was now cornered, waiting for the end.

Just as Anand yelled louder aggressively, the impossible happened. The two demons holding him dropped him on the ground. One of the *Aghoris* had appeared, knocking them out with a brutal double punch. The *Aghoris* stormed in, cutting through the demons as if they were nothing. The demons, seeing the *Aghoris*, howled in fury, but you could tell they were scared now.

Each *Aghori* fought with deadly speed and strength, punching demons so hard they flew through the air. A few *Aghoris*, who saw that demons were about to kill

Ramesh and Gurumurthy, threw some strange white powder at the demons. The demons howled in pain as their skin started to burn, tear, and split while the blood was spilling onto the ground. An *Aghori* swung a Rudraksha chain around his hand and slammed it into a demon, who was about to kill Satish.

While Anand hid in the corner, too scared to move, one of the *Aghoris* kicked a demon who trapped Veda, and was finally freed. She immediately began fighting back, throwing punches to protect herself. Satish, Ramesh, and Gurumurthy were doing the same, fighting to stay alive.

The four demons who trapped us were still on the ground, but I couldn't break free. I couldn't tap into my powers.

The leader of the demons was rushing towards me, ready to kill me. But one of the *Aghoris* spotted him from a distance and shouted, *"Hara! Hara! Mahadevaaa!"*

The rest of the Aghoris began chanting, *"Shambho Shankara!"*

Then, all the *Aghoris* rushed in, started attacking with brutal force. The echo of their battle cries is powerful enough to shake the room. They tore through everything in their path, their aggression was unmatched,their eyes were bloodshot, glowing with rage. The power they unleashed was so overwhelming that their fury was tearing through the room as they killed every demon in sight in a frenzy.

Every demon in the room vanished in an instant. Just as quickly as a sage appeared. He looked incredibly old, his presence was serene yet powerful. He wore an orange dhoti, and three lines of white powder with a tilak marked on his forehead. His hair was white and tied back in a way that resembled a saint, adding to his calm, timeless aura.

I got myself stable and stood up. The team gathered around, their eyes scanning the room. A massive group of *Aghoris* had gathered, forming a crowd, all watching the sage who entered.

I looked at everyone in the room and asked, "Who are you all? Why did the demons attack us?" Then, turning to Veda and the team, I asked, "Why did you guys trap me? What's going on here? What is the element?" Finally, I turned to the sage and asked, "Who are you? What is your name?"

The sage replied calmly, "I am Sukhracharya."

Veda and the team were shocked. They only read about him in ancient texts, and the very idea of his existence has always been a mystery. To see him standing before them now left them speechless.

I asked again, curiously that is evident in my voice, "What is Kaashidhara?"

Sukhracharya turned his gaze towards me, his eyes filled with ancient wisdom. Then, he began to narrate the story with a calm and steady voice.

"There was a kingdom called Vidhehya Rajyam full of fertile land, situated in the northern Himalayas with two sacred rivers, Ganga and Yamuna, flowing on either side. It is near Neela Parvatha and Kula Parvatha, home to saints, sages, and ordinary people. King Devaraja, a wise and kind man, used to rule this kingdom and was hailed by the people for his great deeds in making their kingdom a home for traditions and beliefs."

Vidhula Forest, at the end of the kingdom, used to provide people with necessary food, fruits, vegetables, and a natural security line with many wild and ferocious animals living in it. It was also home to many herbs and medicinal plants used to create medicines. The kingdom's people depended on this forest for their livelihood and to thrive on true brotherhood amongst themselves.

A few years later, an unknown disease struck the kingdom. There was no known treatment or precaution to protect against it. The disease spread with a high fever, causing the body to overheat, but then, just as suddenly, the feet would turn ice-cold, followed by intense body aches. The afflicted would eventually die. While a few managed to survive, many people perished instantly.

People couldn't understand the cause of this strange illness. Desperate, they turned to daily worship, performing numerous havans and prayers in the hope of finding a solution. But no matter what they did, there was no relief. The disease only grew more critical and severe with each passing day.

The kingdom worshipped Lord Shiva, and their priest, Shiva Datta, was revered as a great scholar. His ancestors were divine beings, and their legacy of wisdom and power lived on through him. In his mid-thirties, Shiva Datta carried a calm and composed presence. Yet, when he spoke, his voice roared like a lion, commanding attention. He had a full beard, an oval-shaped face, and an aura of strength and authority.

He always dressed in a saffron dhoti, with white Rudraksha beads draped around his neck and three sacred lines of white vibhuti across his forehead. Shiva Datta was a strong, bold Brahmin, known for his unwavering loyalty and the deep respect he showed to others.

In his efforts to cure the mysterious disease, Shiva Datta performed countless rituals and havans. He consulted numerous ancient manuscripts written by saints and his ancestors, searching desperately for a solution. But despite his efforts, there was no result. The disease spread rapidly, and the people of the kingdom grew increasingly desperate. They had invested time, faith, and energy into finding a cure, yet the illness continued without pause. It claimed the lives of many children, and with each passing day, the population dwindled.

Shiva Datta, a married man, was blessed with two sons, one is fifteen-year-old and another is seven-year-old. A few years earlier, he had performed the sacred thread ceremony, an important ritual in Hindu way of life, for his elder son and sent him to a Gurukul to study the great scriptures. He was brilliant, quickly gaining recognition for his intellect. Everyone in the kingdom and gurukul called him Kaashidhara.

After many years, Kaashidhara returned home, having heard that his brother Kaashi Vishwanatha had fallen victim to the same deadly disease that plagued the land. His mother, Gamana, was deeply worried about Kaashi Vishwanatha's condition. She prayed to Lord Shiva daily, begging for her son's recovery. Yet, despite her devotion, his health worsened each day.

Watching his parents being helpless and him being incapable of doing anything that can help the people and his brother suffering from the deadly disease, Kaashidhara was not able to sleep and eat properly. One morning, Kaashidhara determined that he should do something, rose early and ventured into the forest. There, he sat in deep meditation called ghor tapas, seeking a divine solution to the disease tormenting his village.

Though still young, Kaashidhara was fierce in his determination. He had always loved his brother and had been cherished at home. Despite being pampered to his brother, he remained incredibly brilliant, deeply devoted to his dharma, and a sincere worshipper of God. During his meditation, he recalled lessons from his teachers and began reciting and understanding them.

In the process over the days and months gone by, he recognized powerful verses from ancient manuscripts. Drawing from this wisdom and the educational knowledge, he crafted a mantra to cure the disease.

He returned home and asked his brother to chant the mantra three times. Miraculously, Kaashi Vishwanatha's condition began to improve, and within seven days, he had fully recovered. Kaashidhara then shared the mantra with the entire kingdom. As a result, the disease vanished, and the people began to recover swiftly. They were astonished by his wisdom and power and began to regard him as a godlike figure. Kaashidhara decided to return to his Gurukul after seeing everyone in the kingdom is cured and healthy. Whole village organized a grand felicitation ceremony for him and said farewell.

After returning to his Gurukul, Kaashidhara continued his studies and mastered all 64 forms of art and knowledge known in the universe. He even invented new techniques along the way. His teachers were immensely proud of him, impressed by the depth of his understanding and brilliance. He was friendly and kind, forming bonds with everyone he met.

Years later, an eight-year-old boy was playing with friends in Vidhula Forest. The forest had warning signs posted at several points, cautioning people not to cross into its depths. It was infamous for its venomous snakes, and few dared venture near. The people grew their crops near home to avoid going into the forest altogether.

The forest lay just a few metres from a nearby Gurukul. While the outskirts were teeming with deadly snakes, the inner regions were home to wild, dangerous beasts. Despite their parents' warnings, the children continued to play carelessly. During one such game, they crossed the forbidden boundary without realising it. It was noon.

Suddenly, a massive terrifying snake struck one of the boys. The venom worked instantly, and the child collapsed. Shocked and frozen in fear, the others panicked. When they tried to flee, more snakes emerged, surrounding them. The children screamed for help, their cries echoing through the dense forest.

Back at the Gurukul, a few students heard the distant screams. Alarmed, they ran toward the forest, but as they approached the boundary, a giant cobra slithered in front of them, barring the way.

Fear gripped them. Helpless and uncertain, one of the students cried out desperately and shouted, "Kaashidhara!"

At that moment, Kaashidhara stood in the middle of the Ganga River, offering prayers to the rising sun. His presence was fierce and commanding. His eyes were deep black, his skin radiant and blue, and his expression was calm and focused. His head was mostly shaved, save for a small patch of hair on the crown. Wearing a traditional dhoti, he had just completed his morning ritual, three sacred dips in the river, offering water to the sun.

Upon hearing his friend's cry, he didn't hesitate. He raced from the river, his wet dhoti clinging to him, sprinting toward the forest. There, he found the children trapped and terrified, surrounded by hissing snakes. Without a hint of fear, Kaashidhara sat on the ground, closed his eyes, and began chanting powerful mantras in a deep, commanding voice.

Muhūrtam sannyāsati vā vināśam sannādati, Kumāram damshitam mukti, no chet duḥkham bhavishyati.

His words vibrated through the air, their resonance reaching a frequency only the snakes could understand. His voice carried a warning: "Leave now, or face destruction. Release the boy you have bitten, or suffer the consequences." Some of his friends, driven by faith, began chanting alongside him.

His mantra's power was overwhelming. The snakes trembled and vanished into the depths of the forest. Kaashidhara rescued and treated the children. When nearby villagers heard of what had happened, they were awestruck by his power. His parents, upon learning of his bravery, were overwhelmed with pride. To them, it wasn't just strength, it was divine grace and destiny.

Ten years later, Kaashidhara completed his education and returned home. His parents were overjoyed to welcome him back. When he returned to his own village, Kaashidhara noticed something strange. Though the majority of people greeted him, he could sense some people looking at him angrily and some were escaping from him.

Even his friends stopped talking to him properly. One day he looked at a childhood friend passing from him near the temple and said, "Hello Pratapa Rudra, how are you?"

He did not reply and looked at him angry, moved on. Kaashidhara was surprised and went into the temple. Even the priest was hesitant to talk to him at first but later, he smiled at him with a sort of fear in his eyes and started performing pooja allowing him to come to the front of the queue.

As there was already a long queue, many of the people let it go because it was Kaashidhara but there were few people who did not digest it and started shouting angrily "Respected Priest, how could you? Letting that evil man into this holy place itself is an absolute sin! You should have stopped him and sent him away. Instead, you put him before everyone else and even did a prayer for him. Don't you remember what he did to our village and the whole kingdom? He didn't even spare his own brother, the rascal!"

While the priest was trying to calm down the crowd who were furious and heading towards Kaashidhara, Kaashidhara was shocked after hearing all of that. Kaashidhara lost his consciousness and everything around him was blocked as he could not believe what he heard just now. There were few well wishers of his father and family immediately took him out of the temple and took him to home.

Kaashidhara sat down on the rock in front of his home, unresponsive and rock steady looking to the sky, still in shock. His parents came out and the people accompanying Kaashidhara explained everything that happened at the temple. Shiva Datta seemed to understand the situation of Kaashidhara and sat beside him. Gamana, with tears rolling down from her eyes, gestured the people to leave and stood there looking at both Shiva datta and Kaashidhara.

Shiva Datta looked at Kaashidhara and asked, "I heard you've created a medicine that cures even the deadliest snake venom. But the herbs needed are rare in our region. How did you manage this, my son?"

Shiva Datta stood up moving to the front of Kaashidhara and continued, "Son, I found something that could help you in becoming more proficient in your skill after researching all these years. I met so many siddhas, yogis, saints to confirm the credibility of the secret I found out and they all confirmed it as well."

"What is it, Father?" Kaashidhara asked, intrigued.

Shiva Datta took a deep breath and revealed, "There exists an element on this Earth, a divine force capable of creating anything you desire. It belongs to Lord Shiva."

Kaashidhara leaned forward, his curiosity intensifying. "What is that element?" he asked eagerly.

"The Damaru," Shiva Datta said reverently.

At the sound of the name, Kaashidhara felt a strange energy awaken within him. His heart pounded with awe and wonder.

Shiva Datta continued, "This entire universe was born from the sound of Lord Shiva's Damaru. Its vibrations hold the power to create anything. If you are blessed by Lord Shiva, you can generate mantras even more powerful than before."

Kaashidhara's eyes sparkled. "How do I seek his presence? What must I do?" he asked, determined.

Shiva Datta turned toward a portrait on the wall and pointed, "Kaashi."

Kaashidhara followed his gaze. For the first time in his life, that portrait seemed to speak to him, calling him forward.

Chapter 7

The Other

Kaashidhara embarked on his pilgrimage to Kaashi, the holiest city dedicated to Lord Shiva. Before his departure, Shiva Datta blessed him, saying, "Kaashi is not merely a city; it embodies Shiva's divine energy. He is ever-present there, watching over the devoted. However, your soul must be free of all karmic burdens to behold him in his true form. When your devotion reaches its zenith, Lord Shiva will appear before you."

These words echoing in his heart, and adhering to Shiva Datta's counsel for long journeys, Kaashidhara commenced his spiritual quest. He traversed many cities and kingdoms, gaining insight into diverse ways of life.

He encountered people observing different customs, yet everyone ultimately devoted to Lord Shiva. The constant companion on his journey, however, was the pain of people suffering from various diseases, the one commonality he observed across all lands.

After travelling four days continuously, Kaashidhara started to feel some sickness. He then decided to take rest and settled under a big banyan tree in the outskirts of a Kingdom whose first village was just a few hours away from him. As he sat down and leaned back, he could see a few women carrying pots walking towards their village and there was a group of children playing in the shadows of trees. As he was watching them, he slowly swept into sleep and started remembering his father explaining what happened with their village in the past few years.

After the humiliation at the temple after he went back to his village, Kaashidhara was sitting upset in front of his house. Despite everyone explaining, Shiva datta who was already there chose not to speak anything about that incident but asked Kaashidhara about the medicine he invented for the deadliest snake venom attack.

Kaashidhara looked at Shiva Datta angrily and said "Enough Father. I'll tell you all about that later but tell me, where is my brother?"

Shiva Datta tried to speak something but Kaashidhara immediately interfered and said "Do not tell me that you have sent him Gurukul, I am not buying that anymore. Tell me the truth father, I need to know it".

As soon as Kaashidhara completed speaking, Gamana ran into the house crying loudly. Kaashidhara was confused and also worried at the same time and about to get up to check on his mother, Shiva Datta stopped him and gestured to him to sit.

Shiva Datta started speaking, "You remember the mystery disease that shook our Kingdom ten years back right? You were a hero back then curing almost everyone in this village and entire kingdom. But for the last two years, everyone who was affected back then started falling sick again, and this time even worse. There was no time for us to figure out what was happening to them or why and all of them started to deform. Their hands and legs got twisted and many of them transformed into even unwatchable forms. Though suffered initially the same way but unlike others, your brother died."

Kaashidhara jumped back, shocked by the news. The words "your brother died" echoed in his ears. He shot up, clamped his hands over his ears, and screamed at the sky until his throat felt like it would tear. After that, he just kept crying, and no one had ever seen him like that before.

Shiva Datta grabbed Kaashidhara, hugged him, looked at him with deep admiration and said, "Kaashidhara, remember. You are a wonder. Some of these people think you were the reason they all are in that situation but the majority thinks you are the reason for them to live happily even after suffering from the disease. I sincerely apologize to you that I hid the fact that your brother died but neither could you or I can do anything about that. Instead we chose not to tell so that you can transform and return as what you are meant to become, a great scholar and a brilliant doctor."

Kaashidhara could not withstand the fact that his brother was no more. He immediately left from there and headed into the abyss. He started roaming everywhere, his village, outskirts, forest aimlessly as a failure. No one was able to talk to him and bring him back to his own self. But being a blessed one and a great human, he did not lose his qualities all this long and that made him observe something strange in his surroundings.

Kaashidhara rushed back to his father and asked, "Father, where are the rest of the people? I need to see them and also why there are no women in our village. I only see few of them"

Shiva Datta held Kaashidhara's hand and started walking towards the hill in the middle of the forest. Once they reached there, Kaashidhara could not believe his eyes. All the infected people with twisted organs and bodies were there playing happily.

Shiva Datta started explaining to his son, "When the disease struck again, it came back with more power and hit hard and deadly this time. All the mothers, grandmothers, wives, daughters, sisters have decided to protect the rest of the village from the disease and take care of the affected ones. We arranged their stay here at our deity's temple, Lord Shiva so they can have his blessings and get cured as soon as possible."

Kaashidhara, listening to all of this, looked at the temple and the sight captivated him completely. All the women wearing red sarees, drenched in water as if they came straight away after taking sacred dips from the lake, were doing pooja to Lord Shiva. Shiva Linga is massive in the temple carved out of a single stone atop of the hill and there is a staircase of approximately four to five hundred steps carved as part of the mountain to reach the temple. All of those women were carrying big pots of water and bhasm in both of their hands and climbed to the top even without a small hint of tiredness. With the bhasm flying over and the golden sun rays falling on them, they seemed like goddesses themselves came to help us in fighting this battle as soon as they started the pooja.

Shiva Datta tapped on Kaashidhara's shoulder and said "You are the chosen one, my son. No doctor in our entire kingdom was able to at least identify that disease even by the time you were working on the cure. A real person is someone who learns from his mistakes and becomes proficient rather than giving up and ending up like a loser. You will not stop anything but will continue to master the skill and help these people and the world to be a better place for us all to live in peace and prosperity."

Kaashidhara looked surprised at Shiva Datta and said, "Father, you should be the one more angry at me for not saving my brother and even for the situation these all people are in right now. Instead you are encouraging me to study more and master the art. After knowing what happened and watching all of this, I think I should not do anything for everyone's good."

Shiva Datta nodded and said, "No my dear son. Yes, I am sad that I lost my other son but that does not make me hate you. You are also my son and now the only one left"

Kaashidhara, for the first time in his life, saw tears in his father's eyes and he could not bear that sight at all.

Kaashidhara suddenly woke up from the sleep because of the sounds from the children and realised he slept too long while he was dreaming of everything his father told him. He then resumed his journey after distributing some fruits to the children he plucked from nearby trees.

Upon reaching Kaashi, he proceeded directly to the Ganges River. There, he performed a 41-day purification ritual, bathing in the sacred waters at dawn and dusk. Each immersion cleansed his body and soul, preparing him for the arduous penance ahead.

After completing his purification, Kaashidhara sought an isolated spot deep within the sacred forests surrounding the temple lands, away from the bustling city.

He found a large, smooth, ancient black stone and chose it as his meditation seat. He then commenced *ghor thapas* (intense austerity), this time with a more profound and beneficial purpose, one that could alter the course of the earth and mankind. He was resolutely determined, unswayed by any potential obstacles.

He closed his eyes, steadied his breath, and began chanting the Panchakshari Mantra: "Om Namah Shivaya... Om Namah Shivaya..." His deep, resonant voice vibrated with power, carrying through the silent woods.

The initial months passed in disciplined silence. His focus remained unwavering; his sole purpose was to invoke Shiva. As time progressed, nature began to test him. Scorching summers burned his skin, yet he remained immobile on his stone.

Torrential monsoons drenched him for weeks, yet his chants continued. Freezing winters numbed his body, yet his heart burned with devotion. Years passed, one, two, three, four...

His body grew frail, bones visible beneath his skin. His beard lengthened, his hair became tangled and unkempt. Yet, his aura grew divine, his presence radiating a potent energy that even wild animals recognized. Birds perched near him, listening to his chants. Cobras slithered past without harming him. Lions and tigers passed by, none daring to attack. He was transcending mortal limits.

By the seventh year, Kaashidhara's body had nearly succumbed, but his spirit remained indomitable. One day, in deep meditation, dark clouds gathered above Kaashi.

The wind howled, lightning split the sky, and the earth trembled as if something otherworldly was about to descend.

Then, in a flash of blue fire, a towering figure appeared before him: Lord Shiva himself. His body was covered in sacred ash, his matted hair flowed like great rivers, and his eyes burned with the power of a thousand suns.

Serpents coiled around his neck like ornaments, and in his hand, the Damaru, the very instrument Kaashidhara had sought for years, vibrated with cosmic energy.

A deep, thunderous voice echoed: "Kaashidhara, your devotion has reached me. What do you seek?"

At that moment, despite his pain and exhaustion, Kaashidhara felt only bliss. He had finally attained the divine presence he craved.

Tears streamed down his face as he bowed before the Lord of Creation and Destruction, ready to receive his destiny.

Kaashidhara folded his hands, looking up at Lord Shiva with profound respect. Speechless, he gazed at the mighty Lord. Then, unknowingly, he began reciting all the mantras and songs learned since childhood.

Tears flowed, carving a small channel from his fingertips into the soil. At last, composing himself, he voiced his singular desire for the greater good: "Mahadeva, I ask for your Damaru, not for power or fame, but to create mantras that will alleviate suffering and heal the world. Its divine sound can bring peace."

Lord Shiva's penetrating eyes studied Kaashidhara for a long moment. Silence enveloped them, as if time itself awaited his response. Finally, in his deep, powerful voice, Shiva spoke: "I will grant you the Damaru, but on one condition: you must return it to me in exactly 21 days. Not a moment later."

Kaashidhara bowed his head, accepting without hesitation. Shiva extended his hand, and the Damaru, small yet brimming with incredible power, floated into Kaashidhara's grasp.

The instant he touched it, a surge of energy coursed through him, as if he could feel the universe's heartbeat. This was no ordinary instrument; it held the power of creation.

As the Damaru came to him, Kaashidhara's appearance momentarily transformed. He regained his original, well-built form and handsome attire, yet he now looked even more divine. With a resolute heart and clear purpose, Kaashidhara took the Damaru, ready to honor his promise.

Happy tears rolled from his eyes as Kaashidhara looked at Damaru in his hands, thinking of the suffering people back in his village. Chanting Lord Shiva's stotras, Kaashidhara set off for his village with a new hope and unbroken spirit to save his people from clutches of disease.

By the time Kaashidhara reached his village, it was dusk and people already settled on their beds. Instead of going into the village and to his home, he went to the temple in the forest where the diseased people were kept. He entered the temple and prayed to Lord Shiva. Astoundingly an entrance opened behind the statue for a cave like formation. Kaashidhara again folded his hands in front of Lord Shiva and entered into the cave,

From that day, every night villagers started to listen to the damaru sound. Despite searching everywhere, they were not able to find any clue of where it was coming. But strangely, one by one, all of the diseased people started getting cured. After a few days with villagers left in astonishment, Everyone gets cured. Villagers thought this could be a divine intervention and performed a grand pooja. At the end of pooja, everyone was in front of the temple folding their hands in gratitude for the love and blessings Lord Shiva showered on them, the cave door opened and Kaashidhara walked out of it.

Everyone including Shiva Datta and Gamana are left shocked watching Kaashidhara and his transformed divine appearance. Kaashidhara explains everything happened to everyone and all were very happy for him and their Kingdom. From then, Kaashidhara's fame spread across the kingdoms and even to other continents as well. Kaashidhara kept damaru concealed, aware its power was for all ages. Only his father, Shiva Datta, knew Damaru's secret.

Kaashidhara worked tirelessly, preparing thousands, then lakhs, of mantras for the future, ensuring no problem remained without a solution. Whenever a problem arose, he would chant or provide a mantra, and the issue would resolve instantly. Word spread rapidly, and people from all over soon gathered, seeking his guidance. King Devaraja summoned him to the palace.

King Devaraja's palace was a magnificent edifice, reflecting the era's grandeur and divinity. Built atop a vast hill, it overlooked the sacred rivers Ganga and Yamuna. Crafted from pure white marble and red sandstone, it was adorned with intricate carvings of celestial beings, divine symbols, and epic battles. Towering golden gates, engraved with depictions of deities, marked the entrance. Inside, tall oil lamps lined the pathway.

The vast courtyard featured blooming lotus ponds, lush medicinal herb gardens, and fountains shaped like sacred animals. Peacocks and doves roamed freely.

The main hall was an architectural marvel. Ornate pillars supported a beautifully painted ceiling depicting scenes of Brahma, Vishnu, and Shiva.

Walls embedded with precious gems sparkled in the torchlight. At the center, a massive gold throne with silk cushions stood on an elevated platform, its backrest sculpted with a lion's face. Royal guards stood firm, holding golden spears and shields.

Palace corridors displayed intricate murals. Royal chambers were adorned with silk drapes, golden furniture, and divine yantras. Beyond the palace, a massive Shiva temple towered, its spire reaching skyward.

The air was always fragrant with sandalwood, incense, and sacred chants. This was a symbol of divine rule, wisdom, and prosperity, where kings ruled with dharma.

When Kaashidhara arrived, kings from other dynasties and their ministers had gathered, eager to witness his miracles. The king leaned forward. "How did you discover these treatments?" Kaashidhara replied calmly, "Nothing is created or invented, great king. Everything has always existed with Lord Shiva. I merely found a way to understand and use them as intended."

The room fell silent, then erupted in applause.

Another king asked, "How does the power in a mantra work?"

Kaashidhara smiled. "A mantra *is* power. Without power, nothing can truly be called a mantra."

King Devaraja pressed, "How does a mantra cure diseases or solve human problems?"

Kaashidhara responded, "How does food end hunger? How does sleep relieve stress? Similarly, every feeling carries energy, manifesting our needs. A mantra is not just a chant, it holds inherent power to create, destroy, and heal instantly. The energy invoked shapes everything. A person in pain first needs relief to gather strength. A mantra grants that relief, not to escape pain, but to conquer it."

King Devaraja, still unconvinced, asked, "Can you elaborate?"

Kaashidhara smiled. "King, please have your soldiers bring a dry, withered plant and a water bowl."

Soldiers returned with the items. Kaashidhara took the lifeless plant, pressed it to his chest, closed his eyes, and chanted a sacred mantra. He repeated this with the water bowl, then placed the plant in the water.

To everyone's astonishment, within minutes, the plant regained life, its leaves turning vibrant green.

Kaashidhara explained, "A mantra consists of encrypted instructions and vibrations. Chanting over the plant sent encoded instructions to revive its dormant energy. I instructed the water, a life source, to amplify its giving energy.

The water became the giver, the plant the receiver. A mantra chanted with intention gathers and channels required energies.

The plant was lifeless, but its growth energy was merely suppressed. I removed the obstructing forces, and it resumed growing naturally." "Like all things, the human body comprises elements infused with energy, which can be altered.

Everything operates through energy, and the energy I invoke flows solely from Lord Shiva's divine will." The kings and ministers, amazed, realized they were in the presence of someone truly extraordinary.

On another day, King Devaraja secretly summoned Kaashidhara. No one else was aware. "Maharaja, why have you summoned me?" Kaashidhara asked respectfully.

King Devaraja sat alone, lost in thought, in a stunning room with marble designs and a royal sofa. A teapot sat between them.

A servant served drinks and left. Across the room was a grand fifteen-foot bed. Statues of elephants and lions stood in corners. Long curtains draped the walls; cushions covered sofas; the floor was polished marble. "I don't know how to say this,"

King Devaraja began. "About what?" Kaashidhara inquired. "I want you to marry my daughter, Vaidhehi," the king said. "A curse in my family necessitates a secret marriage.

You cannot even tell your parents. Only after it's done can we announce it." "Maharaja,"

Kaashidhara replied, "I am grateful, but I must refuse. I have devoted my life to Lord Shiva and vowed never to marry." He had chosen a life of service, walking a solitary path. Respectfully, he declined, explaining his vow.

As the day to return Shiva's Damaru neared, Kaashidhara grew restless. He had created thousands of mantras, yet much remained. The time was insufficient. He needed more days, perhaps years, to complete his mission. But Shiva's word was absolute. Determined, Kaashidhara turned to the Damaru.

Holding it, he closed his eyes and played it, sending divine vibrations into the universe. The rhythmic beats echoed, merging with cosmic energy, traveling across mountains, rivers, and forests, a sacred call to the heavens.

As its divine resonance filled the air, the path to Mount Kailash was revealed. Mystical energy guided him through treacherous terrains. His feet moved instinctively. After days, he reached Kailash.

Instead of handing over the Damaru himself, Kaashidhara placed it with Nandi, the divine bull, two days before the deadline. He returned to his village heavy-hearted, his time with the sacred instrument over. Yet, conflict raged within. Had he done enough?

Days later, Lord Shiva appeared in the temple, his presence vast, his gaze piercing. "Where is my Damaru?" Shiva's voice rumbled. Kaashidhara hesitated. "I already gave it to Nandi." Lord Shiva's wise, amused eyes lingered on him.

A knowing smile appeared. "Give me my *original* Damaru," he repeated. Kaashidhara's heart pounded.

Desperate to complete his mission, he had used divine knowledge to replicate the Damaru, creating a duplicate with powerful mantras.

His plan: hand over the copy, return the real one later. But before Mahadev, he could not deceive the all-knowing. Shiva's test was about responsibility and truth. Kaashidhara, heart pounding, declared, "Lord Shiva, I will return your original Damaru, but on one condition: I must remain awake until my mission is complete. If I fall asleep before finishing, only a descendant from my bloodline, whose planetary positions align exactly with mine at birth, can wake me, not even you." Lord Shiva agreed, understanding destiny was at work, and disappeared.

"What happened to him? If the element is the Damaru, where is it? Did he return it? What is my purpose? How do you know this story?" I asked Sukracharya.

Sukracharya smiled. "You are of his lineage." Goosebumps rose on my skin. Veda and the team looked at me, surprised.

He continued, "Your ancestor, Kaashidhara, was no ordinary human; he was a mastermind. He used his powers not only to treat but also to protect. This time, he created something unimaginable, a cave leading to something unexpected."

Listening, awestruck, we grew even more amazed.

Chapter 8

The Cave

As Kaashidhara approached the final stages of his mantra chanting dedicated to Lord Shiva in Kaashi, the distant echoes of his devotion reached me en route to Mount Kailash.

Drawn by his intense fervour, I arrived at his location and observed his unwavering meditation, as he earnestly awaited Shiva's presence.

Intrigued by his intentions, I joined him in a silent vigil that spanned a year. Then, in a profound moment, Lord Shiva manifested before him, leaving me awestruck as I listened to their exchange.

The mention of the Damaru particularly piqued my interest. Upon investigation in Kaashidhara's village, I discovered the villagers cured diseases and resolved problems through mantra chanting, powers, I deduced, that emanated from the Damaru.

Kaashidhara later showcased his magical abilities in the king's court, captivating all present. Seated among sages and saints, I too was mesmerised by his talent. Curious about his lineage, I learned that one of his ancestors had wished for their family to endure as long as the universe exists, a wish Lord Shiva had granted.

Respecting this divine blessing, I resolved not to harm Kaashidhara directly, but aimed instead to obtain the Damaru from him. Consequently, I began to follow him, awaiting the opportune moment.

Determined to acquire the Damaru, I ventured into Pātālaloka, the netherworld realm of serpentine beings and formidable entities. There, I sought an audience with Krimi Bandha, the ruler of that domain.

Krimi Bandha was a grotesque figure: a headless torso with a single eye on its chest and a mouth on its belly. His long arms snatched unsuspecting prey. He was as large as a mountain, with a complexion as dark as a black cloud, his body covered in pointed hairs.

His singular eye emitted a fiery glare, and a protruding tongue completed his fearsome visage, a form resulting from his head and thighs being thrust into his body.

As a preceptor to the Asuras, I revealed to Krimi Bandha the immense power of Lord Shiva's Damaru, a small, hourglass-shaped drum associated with creation and destruction. I explained that its possessor could wield magical abilities capable of creating or destroying entire universes.

I urged Krimi Bandha to seize the Damaru swiftly, painting a vision of a future where they could harness its power to rule all realms. Overwhelmed with astonishment and eagerness, Krimi Bandha readily sought my guidance for this ambitious quest.

I devised a plan involving two demons, transforming them into the guise of a calf. Shiva Datta, noticing them, compassionately fed them and sent them away. The next day, I commanded another pair of demons to assume the form of children.

They infiltrated the household and attempted to seize the Damaru, but Shiva Datta observed them and instructed them to return it. I made multiple attempts to steal the Damaru, but Shiva Datta and Kaashidhara remained ever vigilant, rendering theft nearly impossible.

An opportunity arose when Kaashidhara planned to return the Damaru to Lord Shiva. However, he departed two days earlier than I anticipated, disrupting my plans.

I followed him to Mount Kailash, hoping to seize it, but he remained steadfast, neither resting nor eating, until he handed it over to Nandi. A profound sense of disappointment and sorrow washed over me at this failure.

I pressed on, but my efforts were in vain. No matter how diligently I tried, I couldn't reclaim what seemed lost. Frustration gnawed at me, and uncertainty clouded my thoughts. I had no idea how to rectify the situation. In desperation, I lifted my face to the heavens, my voice breaking with emotion as I cried out, "Hara Hara Mahadeva!" The temple walls echoed my plea, but only silence answered.

My failure weighed heavily upon me, leaving me drained and restless. My mind raced with conflicting thoughts, a torment from within. Seeking solace, I returned to Kaashidhara's village. As I wandered the streets, I observed the people laughing, celebrating, and living in peace, oblivious to my inner struggles.

Their happiness, a gift from Kaashidhara, his magic woven into their lives like an unseen blessing, only deepened my frustration.

With nowhere else to turn, I found myself inside a Lord Shiva temple. I sat silently, staring at the flickering oil lamps, their soft glow doing little to ease my troubled mind.

My thoughts spiralled into chaos, a never-ending argument unfolding in my head. Before I could reach any conclusion about my next move, something unexpected occurred. A voice echoed from the temple's inner sanctum, chilling my spine.

My breath hitched, my pulse quickened. I knew that voice. Slowly, I turned towards the source, my heart pounding. Kaashidhara stood before Lord Shiva.

I remained hidden, barely daring to breathe, as I listened intently. My eyes widened in disbelief as the truth dawned: Kaashidhara had handed Lord Shiva a *duplicate* Damaru! A surge of excitement coursed through me.

I strained to hear every word, desperate to understand his intentions. Then, I heard his audacious condition.

A slow smile crept across my face as the pieces of the puzzle fell into place. This was my chance, the very opportunity I had awaited. Excitement bubbled within me, but I knew I couldn't risk being seen.

Carefully, I slipped away from the temple, ensuring my departure went unnoticed. Once outside, I moved swiftly, making my way to Patalaloka without hesitation.

Upon arriving, I sought out Krimi Bandha. As expected, he awaited me, his piercing gaze scrutinising me the moment I entered his chamber.

Without wasting time, I recounted all I had learned and formulated a new plan. As per my earlier instructions, he had already begun training and preparing a group of demons to retrieve the real Damaru.

After briefing him, I leaned forward and proposed my strategy. "Instead of a full-scale attack, we should adopt a different approach," I suggested, my voice steady.

"If we create a powerful sleeping potion, we can put Kaashidhara into a deep slumber. Once he's asleep, taking the Damaru will be effortless.

We don't need an army for now, only patience and the right stratagem." Krimi Bandha's expression remained unreadable for a long moment. Then, a slow, wicked grin spread across his face. "Interesting," he murmured. "Let us begin."

A few days later, the potent sleeping potion was ready. Its efficacy was unmatched, a mere whiff of its scent could send anyone into an instant, deep sleep.

Twenty-nine days had passed. I remained in Patalaloka, waiting, planning, and growing increasingly restless. To monitor the situation, I had assigned two demons to gather information. But despite my precautions, unease gnawed at me.

I couldn't shake the worry: was the Damaru still with Kaashidhara? Had anything changed? My informants were demons, after all, easily distracted by food, prone to sleep at inopportune moments, and utterly incapable of grasping the situation's gravity.

That very unreliability unsettled me most. Would they fail me when it mattered? Or had they already?

I returned to Vidhehya Rajyam and made my way to Kaashidhara's home. As I approached, I overheard his mother, Gamana, speaking anxiously to Shiva Datta.

"He hasn't slept in twenty-nine days! What's happening to my son? Please, tell me the truth!" she pleaded. Shiva Datta's voice was calm as he reassured her.

"He is deeply immersed in his devotion to Lord Shiva. Do not disturb him for a few more days, he will return soon." Hearing this confirmed my belief: Kaashidhara still possessed the Damaru and was not leaving his home anytime soon.

Determined to act at the right moment, I decided to wait. Seven long days passed as I kept watch outside his home, a simple yet serene ashram built with four walls of red sand and a roof of dried grass. Many saints and sages resided there, holding Kaashidhara in the highest regard. Fortunately, one resident was an old acquaintance, a fellow scholar who welcomed me without suspicion, providing food and shelter. This offered the perfect cover.

One day, Shiva Datta invited all saints and sages from neighbouring ashrams for a grand lunch, seeking blessings for Kaashidhara. I immediately recognised this as the perfect opportunity. If everyone in the ashram fell asleep, I could retrieve the Damaru.

I carefully mixed the sleeping potion into the *Soup*, a watery but concentrated vegetable curry, a favorite among them. To avoid suspicion, the potion was formulated to take effect after one hour.

As the meal began, Kaashidhara, Shiva Datta, the saints, sages, and I sat together. Laughter filled the air as they ate heartily. The *soup* was particularly well-received. Everyone indulged, except me. I resisted touching my portion, knowing its contents. Once the meal finished, guests prepared to leave.

The potion would soon take effect. Just then, I noticed Shiva Datta took Kaashidhara aside. I followed secretly. "Is it safe? Have you protected it well?" he asked, his voice low.

Kaashidhara nodded. "Yes, father, it is under Lord Shiva's protection, hidden far from here. Now, as promised, I will retrieve it and hand it to Lord Shiva."

His words struck me like lightning; panic surged. I had made a terrible mistake. Kaashidhara would soon fall into a deep, endless sleep, and due to his boon, only a specific descendant could wake him. Since he was unmarried, this seemed an impossible future.

Kaashidhara set off, and I followed from a distance. I knew that once the potion took effect, I would have my chance. He moved swiftly, his determination unwavering.

Despite weeks without sleep, he showed no signs of slowing. Then, midway, his movements grew sluggish. He was drowsy. "Not yet," I silently prayed. "Just a little longer." His stamina was incredible. As we neared our destination, he began climbing a steep mountain. I followed closely. At last, we arrived at an ancient, grand temple.

Just as Kaashidhara stepped inside, the potion finally overpowered him. He collapsed. This was it. I rushed to him, moving his unconscious form against a far wall. His sleeping posture was unusual: left hand raised, fingers curled as if holding the Damaru, a silent message to Shiva: "I tried, but I couldn't fulfil my duty. Forgive me."

His right hand pointed towards the temple's roof, signifying his bloodline held the key to awaken him. A slow grin spread across my face. I had found the place. Without wasting a second, I summoned all nearby demons. "Search the temple! The Damaru must be here!" Finally, I was on the verge of claiming my prize.

I commanded every demon to search every inch of the mountain. But the result? Nothing. No marks. No clues. One by one, demons returned: "We found nothing." Frustration boiled within me. "How is this possible?" I roared, lashing out. "Useless fools!" But we did not stop.

Our search continued day after day, week after week, stretching into months, then years. I trained my demons relentlessly. Some perished from exhaustion; others grew crueler, their hatred festering under my control. But the Damaru remained lost.

My obsession grew. I expanded the search to every mountain in the region, including Kailash. One era passed. Then another. For two whole eras, we ravaged the land. Still no result.

The Damaru had vanished. And with it, my patience. For the last two eras, I performed rituals and sacred *havans*, desperately seeking Shiva's presence, believing if he had once taken the Damaru in Kaashi, he might return it there.

We scoured Kaashi, every grain of sand. Nothing. From Kaashi to Kailash, we hunted. Lakhs of humans and demons sacrificed their lives under my command. Crores of attempts yielded nothing. Desperation consumed me.

I ordered the sacrifice of Krimi Bandha, ensuring his son, Bruthala, would rule in his place. Krimi Bandha accepted his fate at Dwapara Yuga's end. But Bruthala questioned my belief. He doubted me.

To prove my devotion, I stood before Lord Shiva's idol in Patalaloka, ready to sacrifice my life. At that moment, Lord Shiva appeared. "Ask your wish," he said.

"Where is the Damaru?" I asked.

"Is it in Kaashi or Kailash?" His reply was simple yet devastating:

"It is not in *that* Kaashi." And he disappeared.

Stunned, I reeled. "It is not in *that* Kaashi."

A hidden meaning. A code. "If not in *that* Kaashi," I murmured, "it must be somewhere else. Somewhere beyond." When I shared Shiva's cryptic message, exhaustion overtook my demons and Bruthala. Despair filled them.

But there was no choice. Bruthala began solving the riddle. Years passed. Then, a revelation struck Bruthala. He recalled Kaashidhara's words to his father: "It is under the protection of Lord Shiva." And Shiva's own message: "It is not in *that* Kaashi." His eyes widened.

What if Kaashidhara had created *another* Kaashi? Hidden near Mount Kailash itself, where Shiva resided. An extraordinary mastermind. A divine, hidden realm. Kaashidhara had outwitted us all. Bruthala's body trembled as he unlocked the code. At that very moment, in Kailash's depths, Shiva, in deep meditation, opened his eyes.

A great hidden gate, concealed for ages, manifested, revealing a passage to the cosmos. Sensing the riddle solved, Lord Shiva turned to Nandi. "Summon him. At once, through the power of Kalabhairava." Nandi set out to call forth the one who had uncovered the truth.

As Sukracharya revealed the entire story to everyone in the room, including me.

Then a single burning question took hold of my mind, "Where is the other Kaashi? How do we reach it?" I asked, my voice filled with urgency.

Sukracharya's gaze darkened as he began to explain.

My gaze darkens as I explain. "After Bruthala uncovered the truth, I wasted no time. I commanded every demon to seek out that hidden gate near Kailash, the passage to the other Kaashi." he paused, my expression grim.

"But the moment I sent the message, urging them to wait for further orders, they ignored me... and rushed forward blindly."

As I had feared, the Aghoris descended upon them with unforgiving brutality, tearing them apart. I sigh deeply.

"A question then struck me: How did thousands of Aghoris suddenly appear there? Where did they come from?"

Determined, I followed the trail of bloodshed. That's when I found a hidden cave nestled deep within Mount Kailash. It was no ordinary cave; it was the key.

When I finally entered *The Kaashi* that he created, the place was astounding. Only those truly sincere in their devotion and life's calling, the deep meditators, the Aghoris, the Naga Sadhus, the true saints, gain entry to that sacred realm.

Chapter 9

The Battle

As I stepped into The Kaashi, the world before me stole my breath.

The realm Kaashidhara had created was beyond imagination, a masterpiece of divine energy and profound wisdom. This was no ordinary place. Only those who had dedicated their entire existence to spiritual awakening, the deep meditators, Aghoris, Naga sadhus, and enlightened saints, could enter and remain here. No one else.

The landscape was breathtaking: endless sheets of snow nestled deep within mystical mountains, where the sacred Ganga River flowed through narrowly divided peaks on one side, while a vast, untamed forest stretched endlessly on the other.

Unlike the mortal world, there were no man-made shelters, only ancient caves naturally carved into the flat-surfaced mountains, serving as homes for these divine seekers. Trees, like celestial bridges, connected these caves, allowing passage through the treacherous terrain.

And the creatures, every animal from every corner of the universe, roamed freely in these sacred forests. Lions, tigers, elephants, zebras, and even mythical beasts like dragons and colossal reptilian creatures coexisted in harmony. Serpents coiled within tree hollows, while rabbits darted through the undergrowth. It was a world untouched by time, where nature and spirituality stood as equals.

Water was drawn from the Ganga for all beings, human and animal alike, providing nourishment and balance. It was a realm of perfect equality. What an extraordinary creation.

In the distance, at the very heart of the Ganga River, stood a magnificent temple, shaped like a grand mansion. But it was sealed. The doors remained locked, and only Kaashidhara himself possessed the power to open them.

Inside lay the original Damaru, protected for eternity.

No ordinary human or animal could enter the temple. They could only pray from outside, their devotion echoing through the sacred valley.

But a select few, those who had achieved the highest state of meditation, the Aghoris, Naga sadhus, and enlightened saints, they alone were able to see Lord Shiva.

And Lord Shiva...

He was far from the temple, seated at the highest peak on earth, where the cosmos swirled around him. Before him stood his mighty Trishul, planted firmly in the ground. He sat upon deer skin, his left leg folded under his right thigh, his right foot resting upon the land. And that land was no ordinary soil; it was an endless field of skulls, stretching beyond infinity. Here, in this divine and fearsome realm, the true mysteries of the universe unfolded.

With a voice that echoed through the depths of Patalaloka, Sukracharya had commanded every last demon, "Leave nothing alive. Slaughter the Aghoris, the saints, and every creature that walks this land. The Damaru must be ours!" A monstrous roar had erupted from the underworld.

The entire demon race, millions upon millions, rose from the darkness. Their eyes burned like molten lava, their bodies twisted with infernal power, their claws dripping with bloodlust. With every step, the ground of Patalaloka trembled. They ascended from the abyss, pouring through gateways of destruction, crawling from every hellish crevice, marching towards the secret cave in Kailash.

The hidden cave in Kailash was the only barrier separating The Kaashi from the demonic flood. The Aghoris, saints, and Naga sadhus stood ready, their eyes filled with unbreakable resolve. But as the demons swarmed through the cave, the air itself grew heavier with death. The first wave clashed with The Kaashi's guardians.

An Aghori warrior, covered in sacred ash, swung his trident, impaling three demons in one strike. He let out a fierce war cry, but before he could react, a monstrous demon sliced off his head, sending it rolling onto the blood-soaked snow.

A group of Naga sadhus, their bodies wrapped in live serpents, stood in formation, their sacred mantras vibrating through the air, creating a fire barrier. Demons touching it burned alive, screaming, but there were too many. They trampled through the flames, flesh regenerating instantly, overwhelming the sadhus in a storm of claws and fangs. One by one, the sacred warriors fell, torn apart, crushed, burned.

The battlefield became a living nightmare. A mountain-sized demon grabbed an elephant by its tusks and ripped it apart, drinking its blood like wine. Aghoris fought bare-handed, ripping out demons' tongues, only to be devoured whole. Sacred lions and tigers pounced, clawing invaders, but demons tore off their heads, wearing their skulls as trophies. The Ganga turned red, filled with corpses, as demons dragged warriors into its depths. Naga sadhus vanished in shadows, reappearing to slit demonic throats with sacred knives, but for every demon killed, a hundred more emerged.

The demons pushed forward, wave after wave, cutting down defenders. The temple, untouched for ages, faced imminent destruction. At the universe's topmost peak, Lord Shiva remained still, eyes closed in deep meditation, as the skulls beneath him multiplied. The final battle for The Kaashi had begun.

The sky darkened ominously. Eighteen Akhadas of Aghoris, each with lakhs of warriors, rose to defend

The Kaashi. The Aghoris, deep in meditation, had not foreseen the sudden attack. Seated in eternal stillness, their bodies vessels of divine energy, they were untethered from worldly senses. But the demons showed no mercy.

Like an unholy storm, they descended upon the meditating Aghoris, grabbing them by matted dreadlocks, dragging them across blood-stained snow. Sacred chants were silenced by demonic laughter. The demons, towering and grotesque, fangs dripping black venom, sought to destroy every guardian. Razor-sharp claws ripped flesh, but the Aghoris, lost in spiritual trance, did not scream.

Still. Unshaken. Unmoved.

Until two lakhs of deep-meditating Aghoris and saints were thrown into a single colossal pyre. The demons laughed, a chorus of malice, as they set fire to the sacred ones. A blinding inferno erupted. Fuelled by flesh and divinity, flames rose high, turning pure white snow crimson and black. The scent of burning bodies mixed with howls of agony. But even in death, the Aghoris did not break meditation. Their souls, untouched by fear, merged with the cosmos, strengthening The Kaashi's divine energy.

Then a roar shattered the heavens. Surviving Aghoris, Naga sadhus, and saints erupted in unseen fury. From deep caves they emerged, ash-covered, blood-soaked, eyes burning with rage. Mantras turned to war cries. Armed with tridents, ritual swords, and sacred fire, they charged, hurling themselves at the demonic army.

An Aghori warrior, naked but for his skull garland, plunged his trident through a demon's chest, ripping out its beating heart. He raised it skyward and devoured it whole, drinking blood like sacred nectar. Naga sadhus, with serpent-like agility, wrapped iron chains around demons' throats, crushing windpipes. A saint, frail yet imbued with divine power, lifted a demon with a single mantra, sending it crashing into the mountain, crushing dozens more. But the demons were monstrous, relentless, unholy. They fought with savage fury, tearing through sacred warriors, crushing bones.

They ripped heads off Aghoris, mounting them on spikes. Blood painted The Kaashi's rivers red. The land shook with screams, war cries, and roars of dying beasts. Aghoris fought without fear. Naga sadhus unleashed divine fury. Demons ravaged everything. Yet, Kaashi stood unyielding.

As the battle raged, my focus, mirroring Sukracharya's distant command, remained on one thing, the temple's destruction.

"Focus all your power on the temple!" his psychic roar seemed to echo even to me. "Blast it before the Aghoris stop us!"

Thousands of demons charged, claws digging into ice, massive wings darkening skies.

But the Aghoris knew; they saw through his intentions. They formed a human wall, chanting sacred mantras that set air on fire. Demons crashed into them, exploding in a storm of blood, fire, and flesh.

Amidst this chaos, my eyes locked onto a lone figure at the highest peak, watching.

"Who is that?" I'd demanded of Sukracharya earlier.

A demon, soaked in blood, had turned to him and growled, "He is of Kaashidhara's bloodline."

"Impossible!" Sukracharya had whispered, stunned. "Kaashidhara was never married. No heir!"

But then, another demon approached, face pale. "His son is trapped on the hill where Kaashidhara slept!"

As he shared the entire story, a sudden realization struck me like lightning. My heart pounded violently, my breath quickened, and before I could control myself, I shouted, "Does my father... Is my father alive?"

A wave of emotions crashed over me, shock, disbelief, an overwhelming sense of hope.

I staggered forward, my voice trembling as I pleaded, "Please... take me to my father. Please!" I stood there, pleading, desperate, waiting for him to answer.

Sukracharya then continued his tale to us, "Something inside me snapped. I closed my eyes, reaching into the unseen. The vision hit me: a flood of long-buried memories, unravelling a secret Kaashidhara himself might have forgotten. After his vow to Shiva, he left, creating mantras. But here lay his greatest deception. Like the duplicate Damaru, he'd created a duplicate Kaashi. From this secret realm, he played his Damaru, forging crores of mantras. Then, a mistake. For one fleeting moment, Kaashidhara's mind wandered."

He thought, "Why not create a mantra to resolve all romance troubles?"

As creator of sacred vibrations, he tried to eliminate love's conflicts, but fell into the trap himself. The energy overwhelmed him, and in the universe's divine cycle, he experienced romance. He met Princess Vaidhehi. A heavenly love story began. He married her by accident, caught in his own mantra's power. Lost in a magical pull, he sealed their marriage; she became pregnant. The moment he understood, he asked King Devaraja to keep it secret. The king agreed. Free from the spell, he returned to his true purpose, unknowingly leaving a wife and an unborn son.

When Sukracharya had opened his eyes to this truth, he'd smiled.

Now, he continued explaining to Veda, the team, and me, "But that was not all. Kaashidhara designed the highest peak, a brilliantly concealed mountain. He foresaw his slumber. When I gave him the sleeping potion, he knew unconsciousness would claim him. So, he rushed to this hidden peak, ensuring no one would find him."

Then, turning to me, he gave his final instruction, "Go and wake him up."

"Why me?" I'd asked, shocked.

He took a deep breath. "Because in your family line, your planetary positions match Kaashidhara's. The temple door can only be accessed by him." He fixed his gaze on me. "You are the only one. Do not fail."

I summoned my power, moving swiftly past the towering 20-foot idol. I placed my hand on his right hand, so massive my fingers barely covered a fraction.

A pulse of energy erupted, an ancient connection reawakening. Searing pain shot through my arm, but I held on. The stone began to shift. His hand trembled, rock softening to flesh.

The transformation cascaded: legs, thighs, stomach, chest, shoulders, left hand. Finally, his face emerged. A sharp gasp. He took his first breath. My ancestor was waking. His eyes, ancient, powerful, wise, slowly opened.

He looked incredibly handsome, youthful, radiating power. Everyone stood frozen, shocked, admiring. He slowly rose, graceful yet strong. As he sat, his gaze turned distant, sifting through memories.

As he had prepared for lunch, deep in meditation, Shiva's voice echoed within him: "Go immediately to the temple you created for your slumber. My Damaru needs time to reach me."

The words struck with unshakeable certainty. Silently, he agreed. After his meal, he set out, path clear, purpose undeniable. Ascending his sacred hill, he realised: this was never his plan, but Shiva's will.

Then, he set off towards The Kaashi, leading, followed by Sukracharya, Aghoris, Veda, the team, and me. My heart pounded with anticipation. I was about to see my father. Yet, a bitter thought: "I woke him. He didn't even thank me. Bloody selfish ancestor."

We entered the vast, ancient cave, darkness swallowing space, a seven-kilometre passage. The tunnel was wide, tall, at least 15 feet, a magical invention. At last, we emerged. Breathtaking. But reality struck: the battle had ravaged this sacred land. Smoke, ash, blood-soaked earth. Screams, war cries.

My gaze darted, searching. Then I saw him. Atop the highest ridge, he stood tall, watching chaos unfold. My heart pounded.

But my ancestor, Kaashidhara, didn't even turn. Focused. Unwavering. He cared not for destruction. Only the temple. Step by step, he moved, aura unshaken, while we followed.

I pushed forward, climbing the jagged mountain with tree branches, hands gripping rough bark. From here, the battlefield stretched, a brutal massacre.

At its heart, the temple was besieged. Demons swarmed, hammering sacred walls. But Aghoris fought like enraged deities, wild hair flowing, wielding tridents, slicing demonic hordes. Chants resonated, shaking air. Blood, human and inhuman, splattered ancient stones. Relentless. Savage. Unforgiving.

I gasped for air, lungs burning, body screaming. I was only a few metres away. Almost there.

As I reached the destination, my eyes locked onto him, my father.

"Dad, how are you?" I asked, voice trembling.

He rushed towards me, pulling me into a tight embrace. His body shook as he cried; my own emotions overwhelmed me. Tears welled. I had longed for this, yet now, speechless.

He looked handsome, youthful, as if time never touched him. But his attire, trousers, shirt, a dupatta, caught me off guard.

He smiled, eyes warm with relief. Genuine happiness. But questions burned. "Dad... what happened? Why are you here?"

His expression shifted, a shadow of old memories.

"Thirty years ago..." he began. "A colleague asked about my long weekend. I told him it felt like a lifetime. I'd discovered my pattern, my genes, where I really come from."

"India?" I'd guess, knowing where this led.

"Yes, Kaashi. He said every human has an origin there, ancestors left magic. The universe itself originated in Kaashi, a place indestructible till world's end. Every human's origin written by ancestors. Yours too."

"So, I could find mine?" I'd asked, fascinated by origins, a scientist in biotech R&D.

"Yes. So, I told your mother, booked a flight."

"Surname?" they asked.

"Dutta," I answered.

Saints took fingerprints, pulled ancient scriptures. Hours, days, nothing. Months later, exhausted: "No match."

Then one saint: "Only one left, oldest scripture. Tells of a family from Kritha Yuga's start. Need teacher's permission."

Saints stared. "Scripture's name?" I asked.

All answered: "Kaashidhara."

A jolt. Teacher called me, brought it from a special room, high shelf, untouched. Long, sturdy. Saint opened it; thunder rumbled, dark clouds, day to night. He asked questions. At last, clear: written by my ancestors. Shocked, frozen. Everyone stunned. After so many years, the real person tied to this story. I discovered incredible things: roots, challenges, purpose of our birth. Too much. Who to tell? Wandered Kaashi for days. Then an Aghori: "Come. I'll show Shiva's path."

I followed. He brought me to "The Kaashi." "I don't want to move," he'd said. "Spent my life here for a purpose, devoted to Shiva. Only unfulfilled wish: to see you. Thought of you so many times." He looked at me, a lifetime of waiting in his eyes. "Been here ever since... waiting for you."

Then, a memory resurfaced:

"Mom, where is father?" I'd once asked.

"He died of cancer. No more," she'd said, face unreadable.

Days later: "Mom, was father not Mexican?"

Expression darkened. "Who told you? He was Mexican. Died of cancer," she repeated.

"Any photos?"

She sighed, handed me a passport-sized photo. Eyes fell on it, chest tightened, heart ached inexplicably.

Now, standing before my father, present time, I clung to him. Hugged him tightly, feeling his warmth, his presence. Longed for this. But then, a sudden flash. Before I could react, a demon's blade sliced through his neck, right before me.

I froze. Mind refused to process. Blood spilled. His body trembled.

And then, he fell. Stunned, unable to scream, unable to move. Just found him... now... lost him again.

The moment the demon's blade severed my father's neck, something inside me snapped. Hands trembled. Breathing ragged. World blurred, consumed by a violent haze of rage and sorrow.

Kaashidhara placed his hands on the massive temple doors, chanting. The towering doors, sealed by his own powerful incantations, adorned with carvings of serpents, the Trishul, Shiva's blazing third eye, radiating fury, trembled, then unlocked. Crafted from platinum, embedded with rare uranium stones, they stood as an unbreakable, sacred barrier.

As Aghoris surrounded him, he took the Damaru. The moment he struck it, divine rhythm echoed, shaking heavens and earth. Ancient, powerful, unstoppable. It pulsed through my veins like liquid fire. Every beat a war drum in my soul, calling me to destroy. A long, sharp weapon lay beside me, gleaming. Without thinking, I grabbed it, knuckles white. Body, once frozen, now burned with uncontrollable fury. I launched myself into battle.

The Damaru's sound filled the air.

First demon; head flew off. Second, blade through his chest, twisted, pulled out in a splatter of dark blood. My movements, not my own. Possessed.

Climbed atop fallen demons, leaping like a storm. Rage took form in strikes, severing limbs, shattering bones. Then, I jumped from the hill. The Damaru's sound resonated, lifted me, carried me. I soared. Landed mid-battlefield, cracking ground. Demons staggered back. My anger, no longer human.

I had become Shiva's wrath.

Every strike, a tandava, destruction incarnate. Inhuman speed, limitless strength. Drove my blade through demon after demon, face smeared with their blood. Didn't stop. Couldn't. Every step, another corpse. Damaru still played.

Some demons, unable to withstand the rhythm, clutched ears, screamed, flesh melting. But those standing charged Kaashidhara, desperate to silence the sound. I wouldn't let them. Tore through them like a wild beast, hacking, slashing, ripping with bare hands when my weapon failed. A force beyond reason, beyond pain. Only vengeance. I turned to see Veda and the team, each fighting their own battles. But my battle... personal.

My father's blood stained the ground.

I would burn this world before letting a single demon leave alive.

Suddenly, every Aghori was consumed by uncontrollable rage. Chants louder, eyes burned with divine fire, bodies trembled with unearthly power.

Far away, Lord Shiva opened his eyes.

Cosmos paused. Stars flickered. Reality shivered. A force beyond comprehension awakened.

Only Kaashidhara knew how to summon him. Born for this. Damaru's echoes reached the heavens, calling the eternal force.

Terror gripped every demon as Shiva's gaze swept the battlefield. Bodies quaked, blood turned to ice. This was the end.

From a distance, Sukracharya watched, frozen in fear. Dared not come closer. Knew he couldn't withstand Shiva's wrath. Slunk into shadows, beyond divine destruction.

But Bruthala, fiercest demon, refused to cower. Rage too strong, arrogance too vast. Roaring, he lifted his massive sword, blade blackened with damned souls. Focused hatred on Kaashidhara. Struck. Blade sliced air like lightning. Kaashidhara couldn't react. The sword cut his flesh, severing his hand. Blood erupted. Damaru slipped, tumbling.

Time slowed.

Aghoris screamed. Demons lunged. The sacred drum, key to Shiva's full wrath, is about to be lost.

Veda moved like a storm.

Eyes burning, she lunged, defying chaos. Damaru tumbled, spinning towards blood-soaked ground. She caught it. Unwavering, turned, thrust it into my hands. Fingers wrapped around it; something ignited. Power exploded through my veins. Body burned, soul screamed. Breath ragged. Blood boiled. Grief, rage, centuries of divine purpose, all fused.

I ripped off my hoodie, tore my tattered shirt. Chest rose and fell with uncontainable fury. Aghoris surrounded me, eyes wide with reverence, bodies vibrating. One by one, they took sacred white ash, smeared it on my skin, marking me with symbols of destruction, rebirth. I clenched my fists.

Then, I played the Damaru.

The sound was not of this world. Thunder and fire. Creation and annihilation. The battlefield shook. Mountains trembled. The air cracked, roared. Every demon staggered. Eyes widened in terror. Bodies froze. They knew. Their last day. Damaru's sound ripped through the cosmos, a divine call beyond time.

It reached Lord Shiva. He was coming.

The sky tore open. A divine energy storm descended, swallowing all. Earth quaked. Air heavy with overwhelming presence; Mahadev had arrived.

He took the ashes of two lakh Nagasadhus, slaughtered by demons, smeared them across his face, body. His fingers touched sacred dust; fear swept remaining demons. Surviving Nagasadhus, saints, Aghoris shivered, skin prickling.

Lord Shiva stood before us, form blazing like a thousand suns. Matted locks danced wildly, the crescent moon on his head glowed ethereally. Eyes burned with cosmic fury.

Every demon trembled. Bruthala, mightiest, raised his weapon, a futile act.

Shiva opened his third eye.

Instantaneously, a beam of celestial fire erupted, consuming everything unholy. Bruthala screamed. Battlefield became a funeral pyre for darkness. Every demon, every shadow of evil, turned to ash.

I continued playing the Damaru, its divine rhythm merging with Shiva Tandavam's cosmic dance. Sight beyond mortal comprehension. Heavens trembled, stars swirled, time halted. Aghoris, naga sadhus, saints, all fell to their knees, overcome. Souls resonated, as if the universe rewritten.

Even I, lost in the rhythm of destruction, rebirth, felt something beyond rage, grief. Divine purpose. The last echoes of battle faded. I stepped forward. Holding Damaru with both hands, looked up at Mahadev. His gaze met mine, deep, infinite, understanding.

With reverence, I handed the Damaru to its rightful owner.

Lord Shiva took it, expression serene yet commanding. The final pulse of divine energy spread, restoring balance, cleansing every trace of destruction.

Battle over.

Demons no more.

The universe had witnessed Mahadev's wrath and mercy.

A few days later...

"I am here today," I murmured, my voice trembling with the weight of the moment, "though I know not who you are."

Yet, inexplicably, I have poured out my heart to you. Ever since I set foot on this holy land, each moment has woven a thread of wonder through my being.

"May I ask you one thing?" The old man, his weathered face etched with the wisdom of ages, met my gaze with a quiet intensity.

"Yes," he replied, his voice a low, resonant echo that seemed to ripple through the air. "Can you reveal your true identity?"

I asked, my breath catching, as if the question itself might unravel the fabric of reality.

In an instant, the air shimmered, and the old man transformed.

His mortal guise dissolved to reveal the divine form of Kaashi Vishwanath. He stood resplendent, a vision of celestial majesty, his neck aglow with a deep, ethereal blue, unadorned by serpents yet radiating divine power.

In his hand, he wielded a gleaming Trishul, its presence both formidable and sacred. His eyes, a fierce and captivating brown, burned with an intensity that pierced the veil of my soul.

"Through countless eras," he intoned, his voice resonating like a cosmic hymn, "your soul has yearned for my *darshan*."

"Your true purpose in coming here was to behold me. Without my *darshan*, how could you depart? The saga of your soul begins now. Reflect, seeker, why does Sukracharya pursue the Damaru? What is the true intent behind his quest?"

Later, Veda and I were travelling by train, seated near the door with our feet resting on the footrest. The area was clean and comfortable. I turned to her and asked,

"What's the next plan?"

"Joining the department," she replied.

"I have a question," I said, voicing a lingering doubt.

"What is it?" she asked.

"After your grandfather passed away, you broke his promise and joined the department. But when you caught the Damaru, you gave it to me. I don't understand why,"I admitted, confused.

She looked at me and explained, "As per my grandfather's wishes, he had already revealed the Damaru's existence to me.

He made me promise that if I ever found it, or if it came into my possession, I must hand it over to Lord Shiva.

To fulfil this promise, I immediately decided to join the department and track it down." I smiled, impressed by her determination.

"That makes sense, but some questions remain unanswered," I added.

I found myself lost in thought, recalling the moment Nandi appeared when I entered the temple during the battle.

I now understood, he was one of Lord Shiva's divine attendants.

My mind raced with questions. "Why did you bring me here? Why did my father hide here for so many years?

I felt a glimmer of hope when I saw him – I finally understood my purpose. But then, he was killed by demons.

If Lord Shiva is the reason behind everything, then what was the reason for taking my father's life now and leaving me feeling purposeless?"

Nandi had simply smiled and countered with his own set of questions.

"Why did Lord Shiva bring your father to this specific Kaashi and instruct him to stay?

Why didn't Kaashidhara immediately fall asleep when Sukracharya administered the sleeping potion?

Why did Lord Shiva cause your ancestor Kaashidhara to fall asleep in that exact spot, just before he could handle the Damaru?

For years, Sukracharya failed to find the route to The Kaashi in Kailash; how did he suddenly discover it?

And what became of the mantras created by Kaashidhara, the very reason for this conflict?"

His words carried an overwhelming weight, filling me with even more unanswered mysteries.

At that moment in the battle, when Veda handed me the Damaru, without thinking, my fingers had moved, and I had played it, almost unknowingly.

Lost in deep thought now about my purpose, I felt a tap on my shoulder. It was Veda.

"What are you thinking?" she asked. "Nothing,"

I replied, though my mind was restless. Instead, I asked her,

"Veda, why did my mother always say my father was dead whenever I asked about him, even though she loved him so much?

If a duplicate exists, where is the duplicate Damaru?" Before she could answer, a sudden jolt ran through my hand.

As I opened and closed my palm, I felt a surge of power crackling through me, leaving me momentarily stunned.

Veda nodded. "I don't know the answers you seek, but I have something that might help you fulfil your purpose." She handed me a large box.

The moment I opened it, I was stunned.

During the chaos of the battlefield, Veda had fought fiercely, blocking demons from entering the temple, kicking and striking with relentless force.

When no one else was around, Nandi had appeared before her, handing her another Damaru, one created by Kaashidhara.

"Give this to him," Nandi had instructed, pointing towards me.

A sudden realization struck me. How was it possible for Veda and I, to speak to Nandi separately, simultaneously, in the same battle, without knowing about each other's encounter?

That could only mean one thing, Lord Shiva himself had appeared before us, just before the Thandavam.

I was stunned. "That means... my purpose is still incomplete," I whispered, gripping the newly revealed Damaru tightly.

She laughed and suddenly asked, "What is your name?" I smiled and replied, "My real name is Diego. But, my father revealed that my other name in scripture is Kaashi Vishwanatha."

She leaned against me, and as I gazed out at the passing scenery, a smile formed on my lips.